Loving the BILLIONAIRE COWBOY DOC

dobi daniels

Luxhaven
Publishing

ISBN paperback, 978-1-958987-07-0

Interior Design by Luxhaven Publishing

Cover Design by The Book Brander Boutique

Editing by JD Book Services

To JC, Grandma D, and DC, whom I love more than life itself.

Dexington Doctor Billionaires Series

Loving The Billionaire Heir Doc

Loving The Billionaire Owner Doc

Loving The Billionaire Army Doc

Loving The Billionaire Cowboy Doc

Loving The Billionaire Boss Doc

Dexington Christmas Billionaires Series

A Billionaire Inventor for Christmas

A Billionaire Butler for Christmas

A Billionaire Dentist for Christmas

A Cowboy Loves the Doctor Series

A Doctor Second Chance for the Rancher (prequel)

A Doctor Blind Date for the Cowboy

A Doctor Enemy for the Cowboy

A Doctor Billionaire for the Cowboy

Standalone

Her Billionaire Nemesis (short story)

Thank you for choosing LOVING THE BILLIONAIRE COWBOY DOC. I enjoyed writing the story of Becca Scott and Max Dexin, a story I believe is needed in these times.

It's so easy to believe love won't come your way anymore because you are in the seasoned chapter of your life or have made mistakes along the way. I pray LOVING THE BILLIONAIRE COWBOY DOC gives you the hope to believe that love is still possible no matter your age or circumstances.

Please continue this journey with me in A DOCTOR BLIND DATE FOR THE COWBOY, which is the story about Dex, Max's brother. You can grab your copy at https://dobidaniels.com.

Would you like to be notified when the next Dobi Daniels book releases? Sign up at https://dobidaniels.com.

Once again, thank you so much for purchasing LOVING THE BILLIONAIRE COWBOY DOC and for meeting Becca Scott and Max Dexin. If you enjoyed it, please consider leaving a review at your favorite retailer or recommending it to a friend.

Thanks again for your support!

Dobi Daniels

Loving the BILLIONAIRE COWBOY DOC

CHAPTER 1

CHAPTER 1

Rebecca Scott never thought running away from the paparazzi would send her straight into the arms of her sworn enemy.

"Mommy!" her daughter, Chloe, said in a tremulous voice.

"Shh, baby. Mommy is here." Rebecca, more commonly known as Becca, brushed tendrils of Chloe's dark red hair away from her face and held her close. Chloe quieted and leaned her head against Becca's chest.

Becca glanced around the Emergency Room cubicle. Structured like a pod in an airplane with its large reclining chair positioned in the center, a computer monitor jutting from an attachment on the left wall, an antiseptic dispenser near the entrance, and a small storage area with wall outlets for the patient's use, the space had a less sterile look than she would have expected at a hospital. But the occasional moans from patients coupled with the antiseptic smell that hung low in the air reminded Becca that Dexington Medical Center's ER was not where she had planned to spend this late morning.

Becca had only returned to the country for a week—after being away for the past five years—and had planned to establish a home for Chloe and herself away from the public eye. She'd enjoyed her anonymity while living in Europe and hoped for it to continue in Dexington.

It was also a good time to build the wedding planning business she'd always wanted, even though she didn't need to work—a few investments had grown her sizable inheritance into a healthy nest egg. But she'd always been great at event planning for high-profile celebrities. It had propelled her into the limelight and given her the opportunity to dip her toes into wedding planning, which she'd surprisingly loved.

But her plans to build a business around it got relegated to the back burner when she found out she was pregnant with Chloe, and she hadn't revisited it since. But the call from Dana Adams, her niece's roommate, to plan her wedding had seemed like the Lord's stamp of approval to revisit her plans and had provided a good reason to move back home.

But Becca had also missed her family—Leah and her husband Edward, and their daughter, Jasmine. With the warm welcome she'd received now she was back and with how Chloe had practically blossomed overnight with family around, Becca was convinced she'd made the right decision.

Until today.

All had been well since her return, so Becca had ventured to take Chloe out for some much-needed shopping at the Waterbridge Mall's Windsor floor, where VIP shoppers received a personalized shopping experience. She'd managed a last-minute appointment there, and the service had been impeccable as always. But then she'd decided to pick up a chapter book for Chloe from the bookstore on the first floor.

It had been a big mistake.

Becca had realized too late there was a celebrity book signing going on at the time. Her anonymity bubble had shattered with the sound of the first camera click. She hadn't expected the paparazzi to remember her, since Dexington was a small city unlike New York or Boston, and she looked different now. She'd grown out her hair in its natural color and had also gained weight after the birth of Chloe—not that she minded the change since she was healthy, and that was all that mattered, though she would have preferred a firmer abdomen.

But the celebrity book signing had drawn paparazzi from the larger cities, and a few of them had recognized her.

A frenzy of flashing bulbs followed. Becca had done her best to shield Chloe from it all, but she'd injured her arm instead while trying to prevent one of the photographers from shoving a camera into Chloe's face. The resulting intense pain had forced her to head straight to the ER. She'd called her sister, Leah Banks, once she arrived, but the call had gone straight to voice-mail. Becca had sent her a text and hoped Leah would see the message soon.

The medical staff had attended to her imme-diately and ordered X-rays and an MRI scan. Chloe had been inconsolable during the separation required for the tests and had just managed to calm down. Becca was now waiting for the test results to come out. Leah's arrival to help with Chloe would allow Becca to focus on getting the treatment she needed.

She rubbed Chloe's back, and her daughter sighed in contentment. Becca couldn't imagine life without Chloe now, though she'd wondered at the beginning if she could raise a child on her own. Chloe had been the reason she'd left everything behind and fled the US to avoid the media as soon as she'd confirmed the pregnancy, and she'd never regretted the decision.

Becca's ears pricked up at the sound of the curtain being swept aside, and she looked up, expecting it to be the doctor. Instead a short bald man with beady eyes stared back at her. But she recognized who he was, once he pulled a camera from his backpack. Paparazzo.

How had he gotten in here? The security around the ER was typically tight ... unless medical staff had let him in.

Becca nestled Chloe's face into her chest and wrapped her arms tight around her. Her injured arm throbbed painfully from the effort. She straightened her back. "I want you to leave," she said to the man.

The man gave her a sly grin. "Not without my pictures."

"Get out!" Becca shouted. She needed help, but she couldn't reach the call button without exposing Chloe's face. *God help me.*

The man lifted his camera to snap a picture. Becca raised her hand to block his view. She needed to stop him but had no idea how.

The curtains flew open, and a tall man in a medical coat over light blue scrubs burst through. He grabbed the paparazzo and dragged him toward the entrance. The reporter stumbled and protested, but the doctor did not relent and soon hauled him out of view.

Becca let out a sigh of relief, and her shoulders relaxed. That doctor was an angel, whoever he was. *Thank you, God.*

"Are you okay, sweetie?" she asked Chloe.

Chloe opened her eyes and nodded. Becca rubbed the top of her head. She'd thought they were safe in the ER, but it turned out that wasn't the case. She had to find a way to get out of here before more paparazzi arrived.

The curtain parted gently, and the tall

bespectacled man who'd rescued her entered. "Excuse me, ma'am. Are you okay?" the man asked as their eyes met.

Becca got a good look at the doctor's face for the first time.

A sudden coldness hit her core, and she froze. Unbidden memories rose up, memories that Becca had tucked away at the back of her mind and hoped she'd forgotten. Moments she'd never thought she'd have to face in a million years.

But now they were back.

Her heart dropped.

CHAPTER 2

"Max, everyone voted for you as one of the top three eligible men for the Bachelor Auction," Brad said as Max typed in patient notes on the computer at the ER's nursing station. Max Dexin and Brad Croft were both ER attendings at Dexington Medical Center.

"Not interested," Max said as he finished up his notes. He'd been on a twenty-four hour call, but had worked a few extra hours on behalf of his colleague who'd been delayed by an emergency but was now arriving in a few minutes. All that was left was to sign-off for the day, and then it was back to the ranch, his favorite place in the world, where he had the peace and solitude he loved. He was sure Bella—his beautiful dark-bay-coated thoroughbred mare—was already antsy, since he hadn't stopped by the barn yet to see her today. So the last thing on Max's mind was a hospital fundraiser that brought him into the limelight.

"Wait, hear me out," Brad said as Max logged out of the computer and moved over to the antiseptic dispenser, where he squirted some of the fluid into his hands. "Max, you are the right man for this. Single, no relationships, and a perfect gentleman."

Max cringed. *Gee, thanks, Brad, for rubbing it in.* It wasn't as if Max had planned to be single by now. He'd thought he'd be happily married with a kid or two in tow. But the woman he'd given his heart to had trampled it at the altar. Yes, right where he had waited for her to show up with the whole town in attendance. She'd sent him a text message that she'd skipped town instead. He didn't like to think about that time, and he wished he hadn't crossed paths with Brad today. His friend meant well, but Max preferred to be left alone.

But it seemed Brad wasn't done yet. "As I was saying, I'm sure everyone, even our dear nurses here, would agree with me that you would be great for the auction. Right, ladies?" he said in a louder voice. There was a resounding 'yes' from the nurses amidst some chuckles. "See what I mean?" he concluded.

"Brad, I don't even work for Dexington Medical," Max said as he worked the antiseptic into his hands.

Brad leaned against the nursing station counter and rubbed his bald head. "Well, technically you do, since you come here once a month, you're on the schedule, and you get paid. Not that you really need the money." Max knew there were rumors about him being wealthy, but he'd never bothered to confirm or deny it.

"You really should join the auction," a voice that sounded like Nurse May said.

Max looked at her in surprise. Nurse May was a young attractive woman that always seemed to mind her own business and had barely said much to him all the years he'd worked here.

"Some of us want a more experienced guy, not some young pup," Nurse May finished. The other nurses echoed their agreement. Max guessed being in his mid-forties put him firmly in the former category.

"See, even Nurse May agrees with me," Brad said, his eyes assessing Max as if about to move in on his prey. Well, Max was having none of it. It was time to get going.

Max flashed a smile at Nurse May and the other nurses, left the nursing station, and headed toward the exit.

But Brad followed along. "Max, you're a rare breed, the kind that's hardworking, polite, respectful to the ladies, and has integrity," he said. "I can almost bet you'll get the highest bid for the event."

"Brad, it's time for me to leave," Max said as he turned the corner.

"This discussion is not over," Brad said. He skidded to a stop. "It would be fun, and a great time to let your hair down!"

Heads turned at Brad's words, and Max quickened his steps. Trust Brad to embarrass him.

But this cowboy had no such plans. Max still had vague memories of what had happened the last time he'd done so—awkward was an understatement. There was no way he was going up on a stage like he was some cattle being sold at auction. No, sir, not him. He would prefer to donate a sizable amount to the hospital's cause.

Max enjoyed working at Dexington, but he would have preferred a hospital in the valley where his ranch was. That was why he was planning to build an ER center there. The ranches in the area needed close access to emergency services, and Max planned to make that dream come true. It would cost a lot, since he planned to use state-of-the-art equipment, but Max wasn't worried—he had more than enough money to make it a reality.

Then Max heard some noise coming from one of the cubicles ahead on his left. He looked around and realized all the other medical staff were attending to patients at the other end of the ER.

"Get out!" a woman cried out.

It sounded like the woman was in distress and needed help.

Max rushed to the cubicle where the noise was coming from, pulled open the curtain covering its entrance, and saw a man attempting to snap pictures of a woman sitting on the sole reclining chair in the room and doing her best to shield her child from the photos.

The muscle in Max's jaw twitched. The man had no right to be here—this was a violation of privacy laws. Pictures were not allowed in the ER, and harassment was a no-no. Who had let him in?

Max grabbed the man and dragged him out. The man protested, claiming his first amendment right to free press. But Max ignored him and pulled him out of the cubicle. Nurse May, who had just turned the corner, saw the camera hanging from the man's neck and hurried off to call security. Max continued to drag the man—who by this time was protesting furiously and threatening to sue—toward the ER exit. The security team reached them before long, and Max handed the man over to them. Now it was out of his hands.

But were the woman and child okay? He rushed back to the cubicle and parted the curtain, only to see the woman calming the child down.

"Excuse me. Are you okay?" Max asked.

A beautiful woman with dark brown hair—who seemed to be in her late thirties or early forties stared back at him with green eyes the color of fresh grass that had survived a harsh, unforgiving winter, yet with flecks of brown that reminded him of the warm brown earth that gave life. She was stunning, with skin the color of fresh milk and curves that only added to her beauty.

Max's heart raced, and his throat went dry. She looked somewhat familiar, like he'd met her before. But how was that possible when he had no memory of it? Hers was the kind of beauty one never forgot. He racked his brain for the answer, but his head only ached in return. A lock of her hair escaped from its fastening at the back of her head and fell over the side of her face, and Max felt a strong urge to sweep it away and tuck it behind her ear.

Then the child turned her head. Large blue eyes stared back at him, her dark red hair forming a halo around her face.

Max's eyes widened, and he froze.

 ecca stared at the face she thought she'd never see again. She could remember the first time she'd met him like it was yesterday—it had been a dreary Saturday night five years ago.

Becca had checked into her hotel earlier that evening and now stood in front of a hole-in-the-wall restaurant tucked away on the corner of the Las Vegas strip. The place looked eccentric enough, which was what she needed—a place so wacky and different from her regular haunts that any thoughts of her boyfriend, Travis, would flee from her mind.

Her heart still ached from where Travis had stabbed her with betrayal. They had dated for over five years and had just started discussing marriage. Becca had thought they loved each other and was looking forward to tying the knot and spending the rest of their lives together.

Travis had grown up in money and was practically a billionaire, but it wasn't his wealth that had drawn them together, since Becca had millions in the bank. They'd met at a movie premiere years ago and had hit it off. Travis had mentioned he'd always wanted to be recognized as an actor in his own right, so Becca had put him in touch with directors and producers whose works she admired and who she felt were a good fit for Travis' brand.

With his hard work, Travis had finally gained success in the last four years. He'd recently gotten a new role for a drama series filming in Europe that was going to aid his meteoric rise. They'd spoken on the phone every day until this week when it seemed he was no longer available. All of Becca's calls went to voicemail. She'd been worried and had scheduled a flight to go see him at the filming site.

But she'd woken that morning to the head-line news that her boyfriend had gotten married to his co-star, who was supposed to have been

Becca's close friend. They'd had a secret whirl-wind romance for two weeks and had tied the knot that day. Travis hadn't even had the decency to break up with Becca first.

Becca had been shocked at the double betrayal when she saw the news, then in denial, and finally became angry at what Travis had done. Once the news broke, Becca's phone rang non-stop, everyone wanting her take on what happened. With no desire to fuel the rumor mills and a driving need to get away from everything, Becca had taken the first available flight out of town, and now here she was.

She looked around the restaurant's nineteen-seventies' interior. All the tables were occupied by folks who looked like they had come there to unwind after a hard day's work, instead of the touristy-like visitors that flooded most places on the strip. Soft blues music played on a gramo-phone in the corner.

"Welcome to the 776 Bar & Grill. How may I help you, ma'am?"

Becca turned her head to see a young man in a patterned shirt with a wide lapel tucked into wide-bottomed jeans. He held a clipboard in his hand and had a name tag with Ryan written on it.

"I'd like a table, please," Becca said.

"I'm sorry. All the tables are taken unless …" Ryan's eyes roamed the restaurant till he spotted what he was looking for. "Could you give me one second?"

Becca watched as Ryan walked over to a table in the far corner where a man—attractive in a rugged kind of way—sat with a cowboy hat on his head. Ryan said a few words to the man, who gave her a quick glance before focusing back on the table in front of him. Soon Ryan returned to her side. "Would you mind sharing a table with another customer?" he asked.

Sure, why not. It wasn't like she had anywhere else she had to be, and she wasn't obligated to talk to the guy. "That's fine."

"This way, ma'am."

Ryan led her to the table. As she got closer, the attractive guy got up and pulled out the opposite chair for her.

Becca raised an eyebrow. *Interesting.* There were people who still did the whole 'be respectable to a lady' thing? Becca had been around the block, and this was not normal behavior. Unless he had an agenda, in which case he would be wasting his time. Because Becca was not an idiot.

"Here you go," Ryan said, gesturing to the chair.

"Thank you," Becca replied as she sat down. The guy tipped his hat to her, took it off, and settle back in his chair after she did. He placed the hat on the table, but didn't say any word to her.

"Would you like anything?" Ryan asked her.

"Just ginger ale."

"Coming right up."

"Thank you."

"You're welcome." Ryan left her side and headed to the bar.

It felt good to be off her feet. She stretched her legs to work out any kinks, and her feet hit a solid mass of muscle.

Becca's face grew warm. "I'm so sorry," she said to the man seated opposite her. She'd forgotten that his legs were also under the table.

"Not a problem," he said in a deep voice with a faint western drawl that tickled her senses. Truth be told, she could have listened to it all day. Then he gave her a faint smile.

That was it. Becca's heart took off to the races. That smile shone a light on her that warmed her from head to toe and wrapped her in its blanket. She noticed how attractive he was with his solid yet lean build, short sun-kissed hair, and a chiseled symmetrical jawline that was perfect for the cameras. His black rimmed glasses, in contrast, gave him a somewhat geeky look she found adorable. But it was his piercing blue eyes that drew her in—warm, expressive, and so full of light yet with a hint of vulnerability.

Becca averted her eyes. What was she doing? She'd just had her heart broken, and she didn't need another entanglement in her life. It was probably best to just mind her business and leave when she was done.

But her eyes were drawn to his hands that played with the edge of his hat. These were hands that were no stranger to hard work, with their calluses, yet she could imagine them being gentle at the same time. Hands that could treat her right.

She slapped herself mentally. What was she thinking? A man's outward appearance was not enough to know the state of his heart. Her experience with Travis should have taught her that. Who was it to say that this stranger wouldn't treat her the same, or even worse? But he didn't look like a billionaire, which was great. Because that would have automatically put him in her "jerk" list.

Get a grip, Becca. Now was not the time in her life to be having such thoughts. Her heart had just been broken, and she needed time for it to heal. If she didn't get a hold of herself pretty soon, this dining experience might become awkward real fast, even though there seemed to be this electric current that drew her to him.

A waitress appeared by the table, putting a halt to her introspection.

Becca stared at her in confusion. Why was she wearing a mask with what looked like an attempt at a Parisian peasant look? This was a real fashion faux pas, and it wasn't like the restaurant was a ballroom or something. Becca also noticed there was a small rose tattoo peeking out from the collar of the dress like it was trying to escape.

"Here are your drinks," the willowy girl said to the man as she placed two glasses of what looked like ginger beer in front of him. It suddenly made Becca thirsty.

"Do you know if my drink is on the way?" she asked the waitress.

"I don't know," the girl said and stalked off.

Becca shook her head in disbelief. Why was the girl so rude? Maybe she was having a bad day, and Becca needed to cut her some slack. Still, it was her job to take care of customers, and a little politeness never hurt.

"You can have one of mine," the man said and pushed the drink toward her. "By the way, I'm Max."

"No, thank you," she said and tried to move the glass back. But his hand stopped her movement, his slight touch sending tingles all over her skin.

Becca jerked her hand away and placed it on her lap. This was crazy. She'd never been man-hungry, and she had no plans to start now, no matter how her body was responding to his.

"It's non-alcoholic ginger beer," he said. "I ordered two because I figured I'd finish the first one too quickly. I can wait for your drink and take that instead."

Becca thought for a moment. She was really

thirsty, but what if the drink was spiked? There were too many horror stories of girls who had been raped after such a drink. But he had kind eyes, and she'd seen the ginger beer delivered in front of her. She swallowed, her throat dry. She really needed a drink. Maybe she could ask for the other glass instead. Chances were he wouldn't spike his own drink.

"Can I have the other glass?" she asked.

"Sure." Max pushed it in her direction. He picked up the one he'd offered her first and downed it.

"Thank you," Becca said, and drank it in one gulp. A burst of spicy robust flavor filled her mouth with a bite of ginger burning at the back of her throat. She actually liked it! She gave Max a small smile. "I'm Becca."

"Nice to meet you, Becca," he said.

"So what are you doing in these parts? Las Vegas is not exactly cowboy country."

Max chuckled. "I came for the rodeo, but I needed to get away."

Becca felt there was a story there, just like she had. "Me too. The getting away part I mean, not the rodeo."

Max grinned and leaned back. "I wouldn't have pegged you for a cowgirl."

Becca placed her hands on her hips in mock exasperation. "Hey!"

Max laughed. "I'm sorry. I meant no disrespect. Nothing wrong with being a city girl. Just different backgrounds that's all."

A faint smile hovered over Becca's lips. Here she was enjoying a normal conversation with a stranger. It was a nice bonus that he was easy on the eyes.

Today was turning out better than she'd hoped.

Becca's eyes ached as she forced them open. Her head pounded, and she rubbed her forehead to ease the pain. She sat up on the extra-large king-sized bed and glanced around—the penthouse looked familiar, like the one she'd stayed in many years ago when she flew to Vegas at the request of a client.

But why was she here? It wasn't her hotel room. That was when she noticed she was wearing a negligee that said "I love you, honey" in pink down its front. She'd didn't recall ever having this in her luggage. In fact, whatever had happened last night after she started chatting with Max at the restaurant was a total blackout.

Max? Where was he in all of this? She caught a movement on the other side of the bed, and her head swiveled in that direction. The bed sheet moved down, and Becca saw the top of a dark brown sun-kissed hair peek out.

Becca's heart accelerated. No, it couldn't be. She looked down under the bed sheet that covered her and saw she wore nothing underneath. Yep, it had happened.

She jumped out of bed faster than lightning, a pillow held against her chest. She grabbed a bottle of water resting on the bedside table and held it as a weapon in front of her. "Who are you?" she asked, as she forced herself from trembling.

The tousled head came into view and turned. Max's face stared back at her in confusion and shock.

"What are you doing here?" he asked as he sat up and rubbed his eyes. Becca had seen six-packs at the gym whenever she worked out, but she guessed this was the way God must have intended abs to look.

Max noticed her stare and quickly picked up his shirt from the floor and donned it.

"That's the question I should be asking you," Becca said, still brandishing the improvised weapon, her voice an octave higher than usual.

This shouldn't be happening. Even though she'd worked in the spotlight, she'd always been old-fashioned about waiting till she got married. It was a running joke among her friends that she was an old virgin, but Becca hadn't minded. Now she'd lost it to a total stranger.

He rubbed his temples. "I can't remember what happened. My head feels foggy. Are you okay?"

"Do I look alright to you?" Becca said, her voice bordering on hysteria.

"Ma'am, are you okay?" The voice snapped her back to the present.

Becca looked around. She was still in the ER cubicle. So she'd been dreaming. She looked up in the direction of the voice that had spoken to her. Or *not*.

Because Max was standing a few feet away from her. She'd never thought she'd meet him again. And who would have guessed he was a doctor, and even worked in her neighborhood? She'd pegged him as a cowboy of some sort, working on a ranch somewhere in mid-America. Yet here he was, staring at Chloe like a long-lost dog he'd found. Which shouldn't be happening right now.

She set Chloe on her feet and stood up. Becca felt a sharp pain in her arm from the movement.

Max frowned. He must have noticed the twitch of pain on her face. "Ma'am, can I take a look at your arm?" he said, his voice reaching into her like it had so many years ago.

Becca bristled and forced herself to ignore his effect on her. How could Max say that with a straight face and pretend he'd never met her before? Was what had happened between them been so unimportant to him?

Well, two could play this game.

CHAPTER 4

Max's breath wheezed out of his chest like he'd just been sucker-punched. The girl looked so much like the old pictures of his mom from when she was a little girl that he'd found in the attic. The similarity was enough they could have passed for twins. How was that possible?

And he couldn't dislodge the feeling in his bones that he knew this woman. His head hurt worse just thinking about it. It had been a while since he'd had the headaches, and they were only triggered when he tried to retrieve buried memories.

But first he needed to make sure she was

alright, more than trying to make sense of what he was feeling. "Ma'am, are you okay?"

She gave him a cold stare and got up on her feet. He noticed her face scrunch up in pain as she moved one of her arms.

"Can I take a look at your arm?" he asked.

"Don't touch me!" she said.

Whoa! Where did that come from? Even though she was a stranger, though a beautiful one, Max hadn't expected her to be the ice queen. But maybe she was just frazzled by what had happened earlier.

"Ma'am, please calm down," he said. "I'm not here to hurt you. Your arm looks injured, and I'd like it to get the care it needs."

"I have to leave," she said.

Max noticed the hospital bracelet on her arm. So she'd at least seen a nurse. But the arm wasn't in a sling or cast, so it was likely that the treatment hadn't yet been completed. Maybe she wasn't comfortable with him there—he'd seen enough domestic violence cases to know sometimes it was better to bring in a female health care provider. None of the female ER doctors were on-call today, so asking Nurse May to see her might be the best option for now.

"Ma'am—"

"No need." She gave Max a glare that was so frigid it could have frozen water. "C'mon, Chloe. It's time to leave."

Now this was bordering on ridiculous. Had he offended her in any way? They'd barely exchanged words since he'd stepped in here, and he didn't believe he'd done anything to warrant her antagonism. Unless … they'd really crossed paths before. Since he couldn't seem to recall, the only option was to ask her.

"Ma'am, have we met before?"

If scowls could kill, Max would have been skewered, dead, and buried with a heavy stone.

She refused to answer and grabbed Chloe's hand instead. "Excuse me," she said.

"Ma'am—"

The curtain at the entrance flew open, and all eyes turned in that direction. A redhead with striking green eyes dressed in a medical coat over green scrubs barged into the cubicle. It was Dr. Jasmine Banks. He'd referred Obstetrics & Gynecology patients in the ER to her for her team's consult a couple of times in the past.

"We have a problem," she said to the woman.

CHAPTER 5

"Jasmine!" Chloe said and rushed over to where Jasmine stood.

Jasmine lifted her into her arms. "Chloe, my darling. How are you doing?" she asked with a bright smile on her face.

Chloe pouted. "I want to go home," she said.

Becca was glad to see Jasmine. But how had she known? The only person she'd reached out to was Leah.

"My mom got your message and called your number, but it wasn't going through for some reason," Jasmine said in response to her unspoken question.

"The network here isn't very good for obvious reasons," Max said.

Becca understood what he meant. An old friend of hers who had worked in a hospital's IT department had explained one of the reasons why. Hospitals, especially the ER, have very thick fireproof walls that are compartmentalized to reduce the risk of a fire, especially given the large number of oxygen tanks and patients with affected mobility. But the downside was that those same walls interfered with cellular signals.

Jasmine turned to Max. "Hello, Dr. Dexin. I didn't see you there. This is my aunt, Becca Scott."

Max acknowledged her with a nod. "Jasmine," he replied. Now he knew the woman's name. Becca was a nice one, and it suited her just fine. Now that Jasmine had mentioned it, he could see the similarities in their features, though in his eyes Jasmine's beauty paled in comparison to her aunt's.

"Anyway, Mom called Blake when she couldn't reach you or me. He sent someone to find me, and here I am," Jasmine finished. Blake Dexington was the heir and interim CEO of Dexington Healthcare, which owned the hospital they were in. He was also engaged to Alicia, Jasmine's roommate.

Ugh. So Max and Jasmine knew each other. This was just great. But right now, that didn't matter, since all she needed to do was get away from Max as fast and as far away as she could. "Jasmine, I need to leave now," she said.

Jasmine shook her head. "Not possible. There's paparazzi everywhere. Security has blocked them from entering the hospital, but I wouldn't put it past them to try and sneak in. That's why Blake asked me to get you. Mom and Blake are waiting for you in the VIP wing, where the security is much tighter. I'll take you there."

That just sucked. Her plan of leaving the hospital incognito was blown. Becca could feel a headache coming on, and she rubbed her forehead. It had been a total mistake going out today. Not only had she met her worst enemy, but she still had the paparazzi to deal with. And she was drawing a blank on how to do that, not only for today, but for the next few weeks till she could shake them off.

She took a deep breath and let it out. She could do this. For now, being in the VIP wing was better than remaining here—she would be away from *him*. "Alright. Lead the way," she said.

Becca ignored Max as she led Chloe out of the cubicle.

CHAPTER 6

*M*ax watched them leave. Ms. Scott was now in good hands—Blake would make sure her arm got the treatment it needed. He looked at his watch. It was time to leave. His colleague must have arrived by now.

His phone beeped, and he looked at the screen. Talk of the angel—it was his colleague, informing Max that he was at the nursing station.

Max let out a sigh of relief. Time to hand over the patients, take a shower, and then head back to the ranch. Since he had no plans to sign up for the Bachelor Auction, he made a mental note to make an anonymous donation, since the fundraiser was for a good cause.

Max finished with his colleague and then took a quick shower and changed into his plaid shirt, jeans, and boots. It felt good to be back in his own clothes. As much as he enjoyed being a doctor, he loved being a cowboy more. Now all he had to do was get in his truck and head down to the ranch.

His mind wandered to the little girl he'd met earlier as he packed up his things. Jasmine had called her Chloe. He had to admit that the resemblance to his ma was uncanny, but he couldn't figure out how that was the case. They had to be related in some way. Max's brothers were unmarried, and he didn't expect any of them to have kids already. So, that ruled them out. Could they be related to his cousins?

And why had Ms. Scott reacted to him the way she did? He'd thought it through, but there was no reason for it. The only strange thing was his head hurt just thinking about her. Did that mean she was related in some way to his lost memories? No way. Maybe it had occurred because he was exhausted.

He brushed the thoughts away. It was time to refocus. His life was fine just the way it was, and it didn't need any complications, not even from a certain brunette that lingered in his mind. Maybe a ride with Bella once he was back at the ranch would do the trick.

But what if it was the Lord at work? Max picked up his bag and left the call room. Well, if the Lord wanted them to meet again, that was up to Him, wasn't it? Max sent up a quick prayer.

But first, he had business to take care of. Max had taken to chatting with Blake Dexington whenever he was in town and had notified Blake on his way in that he would stop by to discuss an important business opportunity with him. The two had met at an alumni reunion earlier in the year and gotten talking. It turned out they shared a love for horses and philanthropy. They'd grown close since then, despite the age difference between them. Blake had expressed an interest in visiting the ranch, but Max knew that wasn't going to happen anytime soon given his crazy schedule.

Max wanted to establish an ER center in the valley and had been laying the groundwork for it. Though it would serve the valley and its environs, he was sparing no expense to make sure it rivaled some of the leading centers on the east coast. Now he wanted to discuss a collaboration opportunity with Blake—Dexington Medical Center could send their ER residents to the valley for a one-month ER residency rotation in exchange for the ER center providing support services—including their helicopter airlift services—to the main hospital. The residents would also be paid by the ER center during the time of their rotation.

But Blake probably had his hands full right now, so touching base with him some other time might be the way to go. Plus Max had spent more time in the ER than he'd originally planned, and he needed to get back to the ranch.

Most folks wondered why Max had become a doctor even though he was a cowboy. As much as he loved ranching and felt most at home when he was working with the horses and cattle, he'd seen firsthand what poor access to emergency care could do to ranchers. His ma had fallen ill suddenly, and they hadn't been able to get her to the doctors on time before she passed on, as their ranch was deep in the valley and the nearest emergency care was many miles away. So Max had set out to not only become a doctor, but to make sure no other ranchers died from lack of care.

Max entered his truck and sent a quick text to Blake. But he was surprised when Blake called him back immediately, and he picked up on the first ring. "Hi, Max," he heard Blake say from the other end of the line.

"Hello, Blake," he said. "Sorry we can't meet. I have to get back to the ranch ASAP. Bella is probably throwing a fit by now, and she's hard to handle once that starts."

"It's fine. We can meet the next time you're in town or we can talk on the phone next week if you prefer," Blake said.

"Sounds good. I'll let you know next week."

Blake was quiet for a moment. Max wondered what he was thinking about. "Max, I need your help," he said finally.

In all the time he'd known Blake, he'd never asked for his help. This must be serious. "What do you need?" Max said.

"Hold on for one second." Max heard him say something in the background. And then he was back. "Do you think you could come to the VIP floor? I need to discuss something with you, and I won't take up much of your time."

His heart quickened. The VIP floor. Wasn't that the same place Ms. Scott and Chloe had gone to meet Blake? He knew the Lord answered prayers, but he didn't expect it this quick. "I'll be right there."

"Could you come in using the elevator where my private parking lot is? A concierge will meet you there."

"Sounds good. See you in a minute."

Maybe this was it—the breakthrough he needed to solve today's mystery.

Max hoped it was true.

CHAPTER 7

"Oh my goodness, thank God you are okay," Leah said as Becca entered the large VIP room that seemed more like a hotel than a hospital room with its pale blue and earth tones wall color and furnishings. Leah hurried forward, dressed in a long-sleeved white dress shirt belted at the waist, her long dark pony-tailed hair swinging behind her.

Becca let out a sigh of relief. It felt good to have her big sister here by her side. She always seemed to make everything better.

"What happened?" Leah asked, her brown eyes taking in Becca and Chloe. Worry lines marked her smooth face as she noted Becca's arm. Becca still found it hard to believe that her sister was already in her fifties—folks sometimes thought she was younger than Becca.

"Aunt Leah!" Chloe said and ran to Leah.

Leah's face lit up at Chloe's voice. She adored Chloe and didn't hide it one bit. Becca had been a bit worried about her family's reaction to Chloe when she'd returned home, especially given she'd made no mention of who the father was. But Leah had opened her arms wide from the first time she'd set her eyes on Chloe, just like she did now. "Come here, baby," Leah said as she lifted Chloe into her arms.

"Hello, Becca," Blake said as he came forward, dressed in a sleek three-piece dark-blue business suit. If Becca was younger, Blake would have been her type with his startling blue eyes and GQ looks.

"Hi, Blake. Thanks for bringing us here. I don't know why I didn't think of coming up here in the first place."

"You had a lot on your plate, most of which was making sure this cute little girl was safe." He smiled at Chloe, and she giggled. Becca shook her head in disbelief. *Another Blake fan created.*

She noticed Blake glance at her arm. "Let's

get someone to look at your arm," he said. "Then we can discuss later how to get you and Chloe out of the hospital safe and sound."

Becca settled back against the pillows as she lay on the hospital bed. Her arm had been attended to and now rested in a sling—there were no broken bones, and she was only expected to wear it for a few days, which was a relief. Because having one arm out of commission and taking care of Chloe was a sure recipe for disaster. She'd been given painkillers, so it didn't hurt as much anymore. Chloe was fast asleep on a daybed installed next to the hospital bed. Leah and Jasmine sat on the couch in the room, while Blake had pulled up a visitor's chair.

Yet, Becca's mind went back to meeting Max in the ER. It had been over thirty minutes, but her heart hadn't stopped racing from the encounter. Who would have thought she would meet Max in her hometown of all places? The man she'd met in Vegas actually worked in her city!

Get a grip, Becca! This was not the time to be

thinking about this. She had an urgent paparazzi problem to take care of.

She faced Blake. "I'm so sorry you have to deal with this," she said.

Blake smiled. "Oh, no worries. It's what we do."

"So how do we spring her from the hospital?" Jasmine asked.

"I've asked your father to come," Leah said to Jasmine.

"Wait, what?" Jasmine said. "Mom, as much as I love Dad, he's only going to make it worse."

The corners of Becca's lips turned up. Edward was an astute businessman who was excellent in handling crises, except when it involved a member of his family. Then it was like trying to control an exploding firecracker. Having him here would truly be a big mistake.

"I was just joking," Leah said and chuckled. "Everyone seemed too serious."

Jasmine's shoulders relaxed. "Thank goodness," she said.

Blake faced Becca. "I think we both agree that going home is out of the question, whether it's Aunt Leah's place or your own. The paparazzi must be all over both places by now."

He leaned back against the couch. "What about staying at my parents' place till everything dies down? There's enough security at the place, no one would know you're there, and my mother and grandma would love to have Chloe to dote on."

That sounded really tempting, but she expected there would be a lot of foot traffic at his parents' place, since the Dexington family had a big wedding to plan. "Thanks for the offer, but I think your parents have a lot on their hands with your upcoming wedding in a few weeks. How is the wedding planning coming along?"

Blake laughed. "I think it's going great."

Becca arched an eyebrow. "Think?"

"As long as everyone is happy and there's no meltdown, I think we are good. Honestly, I just take care of whatever Alicia wants me to do—making her happy is my number one concern."

"That's a wise young man," Leah said.

Blake laughed. "Growing up with Grandma Helen would do that to you!"

The room erupted in laughter. Grandma Helen was a force of nature and was highly respected in the city. Becca wished she had a grandmother like her.

"So back to the initial discussion," Blake said.

"What about my place?" Jasmine asked. "Well, technically your place, Aunt Becca, since you own it," Jasmine said.

"I'm almost certain the paparazzi would check there," Becca said.

"I agree," Blake responded.

"And leaving the country is not an option as far as I'm concerned," Leah stated. "I was heartbroken when you left the first time, and I'm not sure I'd survive it if you leave again."

Becca felt warmth spread through her chest. Tears stung at the back of her eyelids. She had no idea her disappearance had affected her sister so much. "I won't."

"Promise?"

"Cross my heart and hope to eat an octopus."

Leah laughed. "I'll hold you to that." Because Becca couldn't stand octopus in whatever form it was presented.

Blake's phone beeped at that moment. He

looked at the screen and then made a call. "Hi, Max," he said.

Becca's ears pricked up at the name. Did Blake just say Max? The same Max she just left in the ER? Max wasn't exactly a common name, so there was a high chance that it was the same person she'd just evaded.

She shifted uncomfortably. No, that wasn't possible. There was no way Blake would be on a first name basis with such a jerk. From what she'd seen in the past, Blake was friendly to everyone but was very particular about those he kept close. But something in her gut told her it was the same guy.

Blake was silent as he listened. "Max, I need your help," he said finally. "Hold on for one second." He looked at Becca. "I'll be right back," he said. He got up and left the room.

Did Blake just ask Max for his help? This help couldn't be related to her predicament, right? That was like asking the devil to become an angel.

If it was the same Max, it was a solid N-O to his help. She wanted none of it.

He'd hurt her before.

She had no plans to let him do it again.

CHAPTER 8

Memories of what had happened the rest of that fateful day rose in Becca's mind, despite her efforts to suppress them. What was Blake thinking, asking Max for help? But the poor guy had no idea what had happened between them. Even though it had been so long ago, the event replayed like a reel in her mind.

"Becca, I need you to calm down," Max had said.

"So you remember my name?" Somehow, Becca found it hard to maintain her composure. "How could you?"

"Becca, I don't know what you're talking about. I'm just as confused as you are. This is my hotel room, but I don't remember what happened yesterday, how I got here, and how you ended up in this room."

"So that's your cop-out? We'll see what the cops say."

He stared at her for a moment. "Becca, I would never hurt a woman no matter what," he said quietly. "But I won't stop you if you need to call the cops."

"You think I won't?"

A knock sounded on the door.

Becca glanced at the door and then back at Max. The knock sounded again.

"Stay right there," she said to him as she moved to the door. She looked through the peephole and saw a female hotel employee standing next to a cart. "Who is it?" she asked.

"Room service," the woman replied.

Becca dropped the pillow, hid the bottle behind her back, removed the keychain lock, and opened the door.

The employee entered and pushed the cart to the center of the room. "Good morning, ma'am. Hope you had a wonderful night. Here's the breakfast you ordered."

Becca touched the base of her neck. "I didn't order any breakfast."

A look of confusion crossed the employee's face. "Could I use the phone?" she asked.

"Sure," Becca responded.

The woman moved over to the living area, picked the phone receiver from its cradle on the desk, and dialed a number. "Hi, this is Jane. I just wanted to confirm that we have a breakfast order from this room." She listened for a while and then muttered a 'thank you' before returning the phone to its cradle. Jane turned to Becca. "Ma'am, a lady called from this room late last night, placing an order for a celebratory breakfast."

"Celebratory breakfast?" Why would she want to celebrate anything when it wasn't her birthday?

Jane nodded. "Yes. Why don't I show you what you ordered? Maybe that might help."

Becca gestured for her to proceed. Jane extended the leaves of the cart, which turned it into a table, and then retrieved the plates of covered dishes from the cabinet beneath. "We have a mixed berry french toast bake, served with crispy sweet bacon sprinkled with pecan, and hash browns stuffed with bacon, pepper, and sour cream. And finally, a raspberry streusel coffee cake, and berry breakfast parfaits to round out the meal, including a jug of black coffee, no milk or sugar," Jane said as she opened the dishes one after the other. "Does that sound like something you might have ordered?"

Becca's hand dropped to her side. The mixed berry toast bake and the raspberry streusel coffee cake were her favorites and were typically not found on a hotel menu—there was no way Max would have known about them. She had ordered these items, which meant she must have been lucid at the time and probably consented to being in this room. But how come she couldn't remember anything?

"The sweet bacon and the hash brown must have been my order," Max said.

Becca jumped at his voice. He'd left the bedside and now stood a few feet away. Becca hadn't realized how tall he was, and he dwarfed her.

"I'd like to speak to the manager," Max said in an authoritative voice to the employee.

A few minutes later, they were fully dressed and standing in the security room with the hotel manager. Another employee was scrolling through the CCTV footage from when they'd returned from the restaurant till they entered the hotel room. Becca felt her cheeks heat as she watched herself practically drag Max into the hotel room even when he'd tried to be the gentleman. She'd given Max a big old kiss on the lips, and he'd reciprocated. They both looked intoxicated, but strangely happy. But how was that possible when they'd only drunk ginger beer unless … She had to find out.

Becca turned and sprinted out of the room.

"Becca, wait!" she heard Max say, but she didn't stop. She'd embarrassed herself like a fool in front of him at the hotel like he was some predator when she'd been the one that had been all over him. She had to go alone, back to the restaurant to find out what really happened.

Becca crossed the lobby, and soon she was out on the street. She could sense Max coming after her, yet she couldn't allow him to catch up with her. The traffic lights over the nearest cross-walk was flashing yellow. Becca could make it if she hurried, but he would have no choice but to stop.

She sprinted across the crosswalk to the

other side and lost herself in the crowd. She looked back a few times just to be sure, but he hadn't been able to catch up to her as she'd expected. Her shoulders relaxed, and she meandered through the crowd till she arrived at the restaurant. An 'open' sign hung on the door, and she pushed it open.

"Can I help you?" a pretty buxom woman with short brunette hair looked up from where she worked at the bar. The restaurant was otherwise empty save for a few stragglers drinking their coffee at a corner table.

"I'd like to meet the young lady that worked yesterday's evening shift."

"Is anything the matter?" the woman asked.

"No, I just had a question for her."

"Okay, grab a seat. She'll be right with you. You're lucky she hasn't left for the day."

"Thank you," Becca said. She pulled out a bar stool and sat down.

The woman picked up the phone on the counter and made a call. Soon a young lady that looked to be in her twenties came out from the direction of the kitchen area, wiping her hands on her apron. The woman gestured at Becca.

"You wanted to see me?" the young lady asked in a quiet tone.

Becca looked in confusion from the woman to the lady. This wasn't the person she'd met. "I'm sorry, wasn't there someone else that worked here last night?" she asked. "She wore a peasant dress and had a tattoo around her collarbone."

The women exchanged quick glances. "There was no one like that last night," the older woman said. "Are you sure you are at the right restaurant?"

"I'm positive." Becca thought for a moment. "The main server was called Ryan."

The older woman nodded. "Yes, Ryan works here. He has the day off, but Stephanie here is the only young lady that works at this restaurant." Stephanie nodded in agreement.

Becca was stumped. What had happened? If the girl wasn't an employee, why had she served them drinks last night? Or more accurately, served Max drinks? Because the ginger beer had been meant for him. She was now more certain that the drinks had been spiked.

Had Max been a target of some sort? What had been the young lady's motive?

There was no point in staying here any longer. The deed was done, and there was nothing she could do about it. Her only choice now was to go back to the hotel and have a talk with Max, a conversation she wasn't looking forward to. Max looked like the kind who liked to take responsibility, but that wasn't what she wanted. A quick talk and then they would part ways.

She left the restaurant and walked slowly back to Max's hotel. As she neared the crosswalk she'd taken earlier, she noticed police cars with blue rotating lights had cordoned off a section of the road near the place. Becca was forced to take a longer route to reach the hotel's entrance.

"What's going on?" she asked a bellboy who was exiting the hotel.

"There was an accident. A car hit someone, and they've been rushed to the hospital." The bell boy moved on to open the door of a taxi that was waiting at the curb.

A shiver ran through Becca's back. She'd just passed the area some thirty minutes ago and now an accident had happened. Becca hoped everyone involved were okay.

She passed through the revolving doors of

the hotel and walked up to the concierge at the front desk. "Hi, I'd like to speak with Max in the penthouse."

"And you are?"

"A friend. I forgot my items in his room."

"One second, please."

The young man typed into the screen in front of him and then looked up at her. "I'm sorry, the customer has checked out."

Becca's face paled. How was that possible? Anger soon replaced the shock. Was Max in such a hurry to flee that he'd checked out that quickly?

"Ma'am, are you Ms. Becca?" the concierge asked her.

"Yes."

"Any ID please?"

She touched her pocket and then remembered her ID was in her wallet in the bag she left in the room. "I forgot it in the room."

The man lifted a shopping bag and placed it on the counter. He searched through it till he found her wallet and then her ID. He looked from the ID to her face, and then replaced the items in the bag. "Here you go, ma'am," he said, and extended the bag to her.

Becca looked through and noted all her items were intact. Except there was no note. "Was there any message for me?" she asked.

"None, ma'am."

Becca felt a stab in her heart, and she winced. He'd cut her off and fled, just like that. Even though she'd wanted no entanglement, she'd expected more from him, considering what had happened between them. Well, she would grant him his wish—there was no reason for them to meet again. Even if one arose in the future or she ever saw him again, she vowed to make sure she had nothing to do with him.

"Is that Max Dexin?" Jasmine asked, pulling Becca back to the present. Becca hadn't noticed that Blake had rejoined them in the room.

Blake nodded. "I'll explain when he gets here."

But Becca had no plans to wait till then. There was no way she'd put her safety and that of her child into Max's hands after what he'd done.

She straightened her back. "Blake, I don't want any stranger involved in this matter. I can always travel out-of-state and stay there till this whole fiasco dies down."

"It would only be effective if you were out of the east coast," Leah interjected. "But then you would be too far away with no friends and family around you. Wouldn't that defeat your whole reason for coming back home?"

"I agree with Aunt Leah," Jasmine said. "We should aim for somewhere close, like Max's place."

"But we are talking about a stranger here," Becca insisted.

"He's not a stranger," Blake said. "I've gotten to know him, and he's one of the most trustworthy people I know."

Becca scoffed. "That's what you think," she muttered.

"What did you say?" Blake asked.

"Nothing. But he is still a stranger to me. How can I just go and stay at his place with my child?"

"He won't be the only one there. He has a live-in housekeeper, Maggie, who is practically like a mom to him. And she adores children, from what I've heard. I'm sure she'll be glad to help with Chloe. And his place is large enough that you'll have the privacy you need without crossing paths with him. I also think the experience would be good for Chloe."

"I think it's a great idea," Leah said. "I trust Blake. He's a good judge of character."

"Thank you, ma'am," Blake said.

"You're welcome," Leah responded.

What was going on here, even from her sister who was normally cautious around strangers? Unless …

"Leah, don't go there. I know what you're up to," Becca said. She had to kill off Leah's matchmaking idea immediately.

"What did I do?" Leah said innocently, though the twinkle in her eye said otherwise.

"I like the idea," Jasmine said. "Max seems like a good guy from my interactions with him."

"See?" Leah said. "I'm not the only one who thinks you should go."

"Please, just give it a shot," Jasmine said. "You could always come back if you hate the place."

"Trust me, Becca. He is good people," Blake said.

Becca groaned inwardly. What was wrong with everyone, trying to hand her off to a total stranger? Well, she wasn't a piece of meat, and she could look after herself and her child like she'd done for the past few years.

The door to the VIP room opened, and a nurse peeked in. "Dr. Dexington, there is a Dr. Dexin waiting for you at the nursing station."

"I'll be right there," Blake responded. The nurse nodded and closed the door.

"Think about it," Blake said to Becca. "I'll be right back."

There was no need to even consider it. She wasn't going with Max, plain and simple.

And nothing, absolutely nothing, was going to convince her otherwise.

CHAPTER 9

"Max, I need your help," Blake said as they walked along the hallway toward Becca's VIP room. "I have a dear friend who needs a place to stay for a few weeks away from the public eye, and I figured your ranch might do the trick. I wouldn't be asking if I didn't trust you. Do you think it's possible? Oh, and there is a kid as well."

Max's heart pounded. It was most likely Ms. Scott and Chloe. Even though he wasn't interested in a romantic relationship, he still wanted to know more about them. This was an opportunity he couldn't pass up. "Sure."

Blake looked pleased. "Really? You'll be doing me a great favor."

"It's fine. And Maggie would love a kid in the house."

"That's exactly what I said to my friend."

"What did she think of the idea?"

Blake laughed. "She was totally against it."

"I guessed that might happen."

Blake gave him a quizzical look. "You know who I'm talking about?"

"Ms. Scott?'"

"You've met her?"

"Yes, in the ER."

Blake stopped walking and faced Max. "Was she your patient in any way? Because we'd have to end this discussion right here, and you would have to pretend that this conversation never took place."

"No, I saved her from the paparazzi that snuck into the ER."

Max saw Blake's shoulders relax. "That's a relief," Blake said. "That means it shouldn't be too hard to convince her once she finds out it's you."

Max rubbed his jaw. "I don't think so. She reacted rather coldly to me."

"Really? I've always pegged her to be warm and polite. Have you met her before?"

"Not that I recall. But you know what? I have this weird feeling that we might have. And any time I try to think about it, my head hurts."

"You still get headaches?"

Max leaned back against the wall. "Rarely, but I haven't thought much about Vegas in recent times. I wish I knew what I did there and how I got into the accident. You would think all my memories would have returned by now."

"Have you gone back to Vegas to see if it would help?"

"I've tried, but it was no use." Max crossed his arms over his chest. "But I'm surprised that thinking about her brings on the headaches."

"What if she has something to do with those memories?" Blake suggested.

"You mean—"

"Yes, maybe she's related to Vegas. Do you think being around her would help trigger the memories and recover them?"

"I don't know." Max rubbed his forehead. "But it's worth a try."

"Now there are more reasons to get her to consent," Blake said. "She stays safe and you unravel the mystery behind her being a trigger."

Max pushed off the wall. "She might not agree. How do we convince her?"

"Leave that to me," Blake said. "Give me one second to make a quick call."

CHAPTER 10

Becca heard the door to the hospital room open, and she looked up. It was Blake, followed closely by Max. Her heart leaped and her skin tingled at his entrance, two responses she hated but had no control over.

Becca schooled her features as she watched them both sit down in the visitors' chairs. As much as she didn't want to admit it, cowboy or not, she loved a man in a good pair of jeans, and Max had done it justice. This Max seemed more at home in this outfit than in the doctor garb he'd worn in the ER. But that didn't mean she'd changed her mind about him. But she could see Leah lean forward with interest. Always the matchmaker. If only she knew who Max really was.

Blake leaned forward. "Becca, would you like to plan my wedding?"

Becca's eyes widened. This was so left field. Though she didn't need the money, it was a fantastic offer—planning a Dexington wedding was such a big deal and a great way for her to get her feet wet again in the wedding planning business.

But why now? Weren't they supposed to be talking about how to get her away from the paparazzi? Blake was surely up to something. Even Jasmine stared back at him in shock. "I thought you had a wedding planner," Becca managed to say.

Blake leaned back like he was sure he'd gotten her hooked, which if she was candid to herself, was probably true. "Her mother's health is not doing great, and it has been tough on her going back and forth. It's gotten to the point where she really needs to be by her side. So we need someone else that can help us plan the wedding, and we'd rather have someone we trust."

This carrot that Blake was dangling in front

of her was looking juicier and juicer by the minute. But what was the catch? There had to be one if the discussion was coming up while they were trying to resolve her paparazzi situation. And she would probably need to be in the area for it to work. Yet, she couldn't resist. She felt a small crack in her resistance. "I'd love to, but how would it work with what's going on?"

Blake crossed his legs. "It would work perfectly if you were staying in Max's place." Now he was reeling her in and doing a good job of it. "You could talk on the phone or video chat during the week, and Alicia could come and see you over the weekend. You could schedule all your meetings with the vendors on a single day of the week such that it would be a short day trip only. They'll willingly adjust their schedules for you."

True enough. The Dexington name would make it happen.

"I'm worried that she's running herself ragged with both planning the wedding and finishing the residency program," Blake continued. "I really wish she could take some time off. She's even more stressed over the weekend as she tries to juggle both areas. I've been meaning to take her out to Max's place to relax. This would provide the perfect opportunity if you are there. She would be able to kill two birds with one stone—planning the wedding and taking time to rest, without the distraction of work from the hospital, which is what would happen if she was still in the area. She could also make it a road trip with Jasmine and Dana if she wants. What do you think?"

Another crack in her wall. She'd heard how savvy Blake was in handling business, but this was her first time having front row seats to it. He knew she adored Alicia—who she'd first met when Jasmine brought her in as a roommate to co-rent Becca's apartment—and that Becca considered her a little sister. How could she turn down helping her? "Does Alicia know about this?" she asked.

"She was practically crying tears of joy when I asked her a few minutes ago."

Well played, Blake, well played. But wait? Why would Alicia want to spend time at Max's place? "Is Max's place some sort of resort? Why would Alicia want to go there?"

"It's a ranch, Ms. Scott," Max said. That voice again, sending warm tingles down her spine.

How could he still have such a strong effect on her?

"A beautiful one at that," Blake chipped in.

"It's Becca, not Ms. Scott," Leah interjected. "You're among friends now."

Nope, he wasn't her friend. Max had abandoned her in Vegas—he could do the same or worse here.

Then her mind registered what Max had said. Becca's eyes widened, and she sat up straight. She'd heard wrong. "Ranch? Like a farm?"

As much as Becca loved animals, she had no plans to step in animal dung, which was inevitable on a farm. Nothing against them, but she and farms didn't mix. Her high heels, an integral part of her wardrobe, would be ruined. She didn't need to pretend it wasn't important to her. What was Blake thinking?

"Ms. Scott, we don't have as many animals as you would imagine," Max said. "We run a much smaller operation than our neighbors, raising show cattle and horses."

But weren't they still animals though? Didn't they get that being on a farm was not her thing?

"Horses?" Becca turned to see Chloe now

awake, sitting up and rubbing her eyes. "Mommy, I want a horse."

"See? Even Chloe agrees," Blake said, and gave her a small wave.

"Uncle Bake!" Chloe said, grinning from ear to ear.

Becca hid a chuckle. Blake must be used to all the fangirl crush by now. Then she noticed Chloe staring at Max with curiosity.

Becca's breath hitched, and her hands fisted the sheet that covered her torso. She wanted no contact between Chloe and Max. It was time to end this discussion.

She pasted a smile on her face. "Blake, thank you for trying to help. I'll figure out where we'll stay. You don't have to worry about it," she said sweetly.

But Chloe got up, walked over to Max, and stood in front of him. "Are you Uncle Bake's friend?"

Max looked from Becca to Blake, and then back to Chloe. "Yes."

Chloe nodded with all seriousness, like Max had passed some test. "Hello, my name is Chloe. What's your name?"

"I'm Max."

"Like Max the dog?' The room erupted in laughter. "I like Max the dog," she said.

"Okay. Yes, Max like Max the dog," he confirmed. He gave Chloe a smile.

Good on Max for playing along, but that didn't change her opinion of him.

"Do you have a horse?" Chloe asked him.

This was not good. Chloe didn't let up for days, even weeks, when she was fascinated by something, and then she would forget about them like they'd never been on her radar. Becca had forgotten that her latest fixation was on horses.

"Yes, I do. Lots of them. Do you want to see them?"

Chloe nodded enthusiastically.

Becca's heart sank. When she'd decided on not having anything to do with Max, she hadn't accounted for Chloe's reaction. Chloe was the only person who could break down all Becca's walls. Becca could already guess how everything was going to play out, but there was nothing she could do to stop it.

Max leaned forward. "Can I tell you a secret?"

Chloe nodded, her big blue eyes all solemn.

"I'd like you and your mom to come and visit my place," Max said.

"And see the horse?"

"And see the horse too. Her name is Bella."

Chloe rushed to Becca, her whole body a ball of excitement as she tugged at her arm. "Mommy, can we go? Please?"

Becca glanced at Max and Blake. Blake avoided eye contact and pretended to brush some invisible lint from his suit, while Max stared back at her with a calm demeanor, yet with an open challenge in his eyes. They'd played the Chloe card, the one sure card that would sway her decision.

"Please, Mommy," Chloe begged. Becca could already see the beginnings of what could potentially snowball into a full tantrum. At this point, she had no choice.

"Okay, sweetheart. We'll go, but only for a few days." She would stay there long enough to make Chloe happy, and then she was out of there.

"Yay!" Chloe said, jumping up and down.

Becca sighed. Now she had no choice but to deal with the jerk for a few more days.

CHAPTER 11

Max hadn't expected Becca to give in, but he'd been pleased when she did. Now, all he needed to do was spend enough time with her and Chloe, and maybe, just maybe, he'd unravel the mystery of why she triggered his headaches and why Chloe looked so much like his mother.

He could even say he was very excited, which was unusual in itself. He'd only met her today as far as he remembered, and she'd been frigid with him. So why was he drawn to her? It wasn't like he was looking for a relationship, though the thought of it did not send him running for the hills. Which was strange because

Max was allergic to relationships, which hadn't always been the case.

Max had been engaged to marry before. He'd met Tammy on a cold rainy day. She was walking to school with her bag over her head, and he'd offered her his umbrella. She'd insisted they share, and they'd stuck together ever since. Tammy was a big believer in living out one's dreams, so she and Max had agreed they would finish college and work for a few years before getting married. The road to get there had been long, since Tammy chose to become a veterinarian while Max selected medicine. But they'd worked hard at their relationship, and it was stronger than ever when Max had proposed.

Tammy accepted with tears in her eyes. She threw herself into the wedding planning with so much gusto that Max wondered if she'd been expecting the proposal for a long time despite their agreement. But he was glad he was going to spend the rest of his life with her. So imagine his shock when she jilted him at the altar, leaving a note that she'd skipped town with one of his temporary ranch hands, since she didn't want to stay any longer in the hick town. But he'd found it hard to believe and planned to track her down to find out the truth.

Then the rumors had spread through town that Tammy had skipped with Rex, Max's younger brother. Different folks recalled seeing them together. Rex had disappeared at the same time and hadn't been back since. Rex had always been the hotheaded one, and he had a deep crush on Tammy, but Max had never imagined his own brother would stab him in the back.

Max had closed his heart ever since and remained content with his ranch and his horses. He'd lost interest in any romantic entanglements. The mothers in town tried to hook him up with their daughters, but he kept declining and soon they stopped asking. So he was surprised at his reaction to Becca. All he had to do now was quickly cart her away to his ranch before she changed her mind.

Max stood up. "Can I have your car keys?" he asked Becca.

Becca narrowed her gaze at him. "What for?"

"To grab Chloe's car seat."

A look of surprise crossed her face. "Oh."

"Don't move," Leah said. "I'll get them." She

moved over to the bedside table and rummaged in Becca's bag, which had been placed in its deep drawer. She found the keys and handed them over to Max. "It's a white Audi SUV."

"Thank you," Max said.

"You're welcome. I'll need your address to send some of Becca's things down."

"Sure thing. I'll hand it to you before I leave."

"Take good care of her. I'll hurt you if anything happens to her," she said with a smile on her face. But Max could see she meant every word of it.

He nodded. "I will."

"Do you know how to install a car seat?" Becca asked.

"No, but it shouldn't be too hard," Max said. He thought he saw a corner of Becca's lip turn up, but he couldn't bet on it.

Max left the VIP wing and headed down to the parking lot. He noticed the throng of paparazzi still hanging around and prayed none of them would realize he was going to Becca's car. He found the SUV easily, and luckily there were no reporters in its vicinity.

Max extracted the car seat, relocked the car,

and moved away quickly. He soon reached the garage where his truck was parked and proceeded to install the seat.

Thirty minutes and a bucketload of sweat later, the car seat was in place. He hadn't expected it to be this hard. He was used to fixing equipment around the ranch and saddling up horses, but installing the car seat was much more difficult than both activities combined. He'd ended up searching on the internet for a video to guide him, since Chloe's safety was paramount. Becca would also skin him alive if he made a mistake.

Becca. Just the thought of her name excited him. It had been too many years since he'd felt this way towards a woman. Thank goodness he hadn't been the only ER attending-on-duty, otherwise she would have been his patient, and he would have lost the chance to get to know her more.

He checked the installation of the car seat one more time.

Now all that was left was for it to pass the Mama Bear test.

CHAPTER 12

Max's truck was parked in the Dexington family private parking spot, which was screened from prying eyes, so there were no reporters hanging around. The truck was large and easily dwarfed Becca's SUV. It was cleaner than she'd expected for a guy's vehicle.

She inspected the car seat that Max had installed. *Interesting.* He'd managed to set it up correctly, which was a feat, considering he was single—well, she'd checked and he had no ring or ring marks on his finger. He'd done a fine job, but that didn't mean she'd changed her mind about the kind of person he was.

"It's fine," she said finally. Max gave her a

small smile which she forced herself to ignore, though it was hard to suppress how it made her body hum with excitement.

Blake, who'd been carrying Chloe the whole time, moved to put her in the car.

"Let me," Max said, and Blake handed Chloe over to him. Becca watched as Max tucked her into the car seat, securing her correctly. Since there was no luggage, all that was left was for Becca to get in the vehicle, and then they would be on their way.

Becca moved to the other side of the truck so she could share the back seat with Chloe, but Max got there faster and opened the door for her.

It was a nice gesture, but she didn't need his help.

When he proceeded to assist her into the vehicle, Becca scowled at him. Once was enough for someone she wasn't enamored with.

Max backed down and made way for her.

Becca used her good arm to climb into the truck. Leah handed her her handbag, and she placed it beside her.

She waved goodbye to Leah, Blake, and Jasmine as Max entered the driver's seat. He picked up a cowboy hat that had been on the front passenger seat and plopped it on his head. Now he really looked like a man from the country.

Leah had gotten Max's address, and she promised again to send Becca's things over the next day—the risk of getting caught by the paparazzi was still too high, so they couldn't stop by on their way and pick it up themselves. The truck rolled out of the garage and into the street using the owner's private exit.

This was really happening. If anyone had told her she would one day be in a car on her way to Max's place, she would have laughed them off. Yet, here she was, riding into the lion's den.

Chloe soon fell asleep, and Becca didn't know when she dozed off. She opened her eyes to see that the truck was no longer moving. She checked the time on her phone—she'd slept for a few hours, and she felt bad about it. But that didn't change the reality that they had arrived.

Then she took a look at her surroundings and gasped. The truck stood in front of the most picturesque place she had ever seen, the sort she'd always assumed only existed in storybooks. It was a sprawling log-and-stone house that had both vintage and modern features, with a long driveway made of stones of various colors.

A large expanse of manicured lawn surrounded the house. Bursts of color from flowering meadows stretched out in the background as far as her eyes could see, interspersed with what looked like streams of shimmering water making their merry way through them. Towering mountains in the distance completed the image. It truly was a jewel in the valley and would make a great background for wedding pictures. If this was a small ranch, Becca wondered how big the other ranches were.

Max got out of the truck and Becca followed suit before he had a chance to open the door for her. She took a deep breath and inhaled the fresh spring air—she had to admit that it was different from that in the city.

The front door to the house burst open, and a buxom woman with short silvery hair came into view. She wore a warm smile and came around to give Becca a hug. "Welcome to Dexin Ranch, my dear," she said. "I'm Maggie."

Becca returned her hug, and Maggie's scent

of cinnamon and spice enveloped her. "Thank you," Becca said, taking a liking to her. "I'm Becca. You have a lovely place."

Maggie released her and beamed. "The boys and their mother made it this way. It's God's own place on earth, I reckon."

Then Becca noticed a large rustic-styled building not too far away on the left. "What is that place?" she asked.

"It's the barn where we keep some of the horses," Max said from behind her. He'd extracted Chloe from her car seat and now led the way to a smaller entrance on the side of the house.

Becca glanced at the building again. Maybe she'd get a chance to ride one of the horses.

She followed Max into the home, and they entered a small room. A log bench rested along the wall, and rows of worn boots sat on low shelfs. There were hanging racks for jackets and raincoats and a spot for umbrellas too. A few closets were set into one side of the wall, meeting the marble flooring that covered the length of the room.

"This is the mudroom," Max said. "We tend to use this entrance the most so we don't track mud in." And then he led the way into the main house.

Becca's eyes widened. Whoever had decorated this home was a genius. Elements of log and stone were fully integrated into the design of the home, giving it a rugged look. Yet it was warm, inviting, and homey. "This is beautiful," she said.

"Thank you," Max responded. "My mother loved decorating."

"Mommy?" Chloe asked.

Becca saw she was finally awake. The girl clamored to be released, and Max set her down. She ran to Becca and hid behind her.

Maggie approached her and stooped to her level. "What's your name, sweetheart?" Maggie asked.

"Chloe," she said shyly.

"I'm Maggie." Maggie opened her arms and Chloe stepped in and hugged her back. "Good girl." Then she released her. Maggie turned to Max. "I think you should take Becca and Chloe to their room so they can freshen up."

"This way," Max said, and lifted Chloe back into his arms.

Chloe giggled and smiled at Becca.

Max led Becca up a log-hewn winding stair-case till they got to the second floor, and then down the hallway on the right to the room at the end. Max opened the door to a magnificent room decorated in pale blue and pink, one she wouldn't have expected in such a house.

"Do you have a sister?" Becca asked.

"Nope. Three younger brothers. They each have their own place on other parts of the property. But Maggie insists we all eat our meals together, so you'll meet two of them for dinner. The third isn't around. Why do you ask?" He placed Chloe down on her feet.

Becca waved her arm round the place. "Because this is obviously a girl's room."

His striking blue eyes assessed her. "Ma always wished for a girl. When she didn't have one, she decorated a room instead. Maggie and I thought it would be perfect for you and Chloe."

He turned and opened a door in the room. "There are some clothes in here, and you're welcome to use them as you please."

Becca stepped through the door to see a walk-in-closet that rivaled the size of hers at home. Clothes that looked to be her size were lined up on one side of the wall with Chloe's size on the other side. "What's this?" she asked.

Max's ears turned red. "I called Maggie on our way in and asked her to take care of it."

"But how did you know our sizes?" Because the clothes looked like they belonged to Becca and Chloe.

"Leah told me, and I sent Maggie the details."

She should have known Leah the matchmaker was at work.

"I hope it wasn't intrusive of me," Max continued. "I just wanted to make sure you had what you needed till your things arrived."

Becca was silent. It was a little over-the-top but was thoughtful. "Thank you," she said quietly.

The air between them sizzled with electricity. Max stood close to her, and his woodsy peppermint smell filled her nostrils and tickled her insides. Max must have felt the same, because he cleared his throat and said. "I'll leave you to rest and will see you later for dinner. We'll talk after that." He didn't wait for her response and left the room, shutting the door quietly behind him.

Becca checked out the rest of the space.

Chloe discovered a side parlor filled with toys she could play with. Another door led to a luxuriant bathroom with a sky view.

Becca strolled back to the bedroom and dropped her bag on the large king-sized bed and removed her shoes. The hard floor was warm to touch. *They must be heated*, she thought. She laid back on the bed. It was soft, fluffy, but firm, just the way she liked it. Chloe jumped up and down on the bed in excitement.

Becca sent a quick text to Leah to let her know she'd arrived safely. Then she took a luxurious bath in the jacuzzi with Chloe, the jets pampering her skin. Once she was done, she changed into a maxi dress she'd been drawn to. The material was silky and soft to touch and was of the highest quality. It must have cost a lot, and she wondered how Max had managed that on a doctor's salary. She found a simple frock for Chloe that suited her perfectly.

A knock sounded on the door.

"Come in," Becca said.

It was Maggie. "Is everything to your liking?" she asked.

Becca gave her a warm smile. "Thank you for the clothes."

Maggie beamed. "Believe me, I enjoyed shopping for them. I've only ever bought boy clothes. This was fun."

"Do you have a mall nearby?"

"No, I took the helicopter to New York and back."

Helicopter? What was Maggie talking about? "You have a helicopter on the ranch?"

"Yes, there is a helipad somewhere on the property."

The ranch must be richer than she imagined for them to have a helicopter.

"You look tired," Maggie said. "Why don't you take a nap?"

"I slept on the way over," Becca said.

"You should grab some more sleep. Trust me, that arm needs rest for it to heal," she said in a voice that brokered no argument. "We'll have dinner once you wake up. Chloe can come and bake cookies with me till then. Would you like that, Chloe?"

Chloe nodded enthusiastically. "Mommy?"

"Okay, you can go, sweetheart," Becca said with a smile.

"Yay!"

Maggie held out her hand to Chloe. "Let's go."

Chloe bounced off the bed and took the proffered hand.

Becca watched them leave. It was interesting to see Chloe take to strangers, unlike herself.

She laid back on the bed. She couldn't believe she was in Max's house. He'd been the perfect gentleman so far, but that didn't mean she'd let down her guard and trust him—the jury was still out on that one.

But how could he be so different from the man she'd met in Vegas, the man that had abandoned her? People never changed that easily. She had a feeling this was too good to be true, but for now she would stay on alert and watch.

Maggie must have been right, because Becca drifted off to sleep as soon as her head hit the pillow.

Becca woke up to a darkened room. She initially panicked at the unfamiliar surroundings, but then she remembered where she was. She reached for her phone on the bedside table and checked the time. She'd slept longer than she'd planned and was probably late for dinner. She got up, washed her face, and hurried down.

Maggie looked up with a smile at her descent. They were seated around a large farmhouse dining table, with Max at the head. And there were two other men who shared the same facial features as Max seated on his left. "I was about to come and get you," she said and gestured to the space next to where Chloe sat on Max's right. Becca slid into the space and acknowledged Max with a nod. She hated to admit that the man looked delicious in a cream Henley paired with blue jeans.

The younger of the two men and the blond version greeted her with a warm smile. "I'm Jax, and this is my brother, Dex. And yes, Ma had a love for the letter x," he said as he gestured to the older and larger version who assessed Becca cooly.

"Nice to meet you," Becca said with a small smile.

"Welcome to our home," Jax said. "Wow, I have to say Chloe looks a bit like our mom. Dex, wouldn't you agree?"

Dex grunted his assent.

"He's a man of few words," Maggie said to Becca.

The comparison to their mother's likeness was interesting. Max hadn't mentioned anything about it. Was that why he had looked at Chloe the way he did when they'd first met?

Jax wasn't finished. "You are the first woman Max has brought home since—"

"Okay, let's eat," Maggie said.

Becca wondered what Jax had been about to say. She noted Max didn't respond to the comment and instead led them in a short prayer before they dove in.

The food was excellent. There was smoky cheddar mac and cheese, ribeye steak in a creamy sauce, a potato dish with carrots and mushrooms, and maple bacon baked beans. Dessert was topped off with the cookies that Chloe had helped bake. Becca would have to be careful, or else she would end up with an expanded waistline. The guys tucked in so much food she wondered where they fit it all. But they were lean with no fat in sight, and she figured the ranch activities demanded that much of them.

Dex and Jax talked about the work they'd

accomplished for the day, and it was fascinating to watch Max's depth of knowledge and wisdom that he shared without seeming to impose his decisions on them. It turned out Dex managed the day-to-day operations of the ranch, while Jax was the financial brain of the operation. Maggie had to make them stop, and Jax turned to telling Chloe long tales about the horses on the farm.

Becca had never seen Chloe laugh so much, and she had to make sure she ate enough. Max stayed attentive to Chloe, putting whatever she wanted within reach. By the time dinner was done, Max had promised Chloe he'd take her to see the horses the next day. Dex, on the other hand, seemed to study Becca throughout the dinner but said nothing to her. Dinner was delicious, and she said as much to Maggie.

"Thank you," Maggie responded, her pleasure at the remark written all over her face.

When dinner was over, the guys cleared the table.

"What can I do to help?" Becca asked.

"We can handle it," Jax said.

"Are you sure?" Becca said.

Jax lowered his voice. "We have to, otherwise

we might get a whooping from Maggie," he said and winked at her.

Becca laughed, and she felt eyes on her. She turned to see Max staring at her from where he stood at the sink.

Her face heated, and she averted her eyes. Why was he looking at her like he was about to gobble her up? He was only her enemy, pure and simple, though she sensed her heart was in conflict about it.

"Okay, I'll make coffee instead," she said. "How do you guys like it?"

"Black with no cream or sugar for all of us," Jax answered.

Just like she did. She found what she needed on the kitchen island, and the smell of roasted coffee beans soon filled the air.

The dishes were done in no time, and Jax and Dex took their coffee and wandered off to another part of the house. Becca sipped hers as she leaned against the island countertop and watched Maggie engage Chloe in a puzzle on the floor of the living room.

Then she sensed Max's presence beside her, heralded by the familiar scent that sent the butterflies in her stomach spinning.

"Can we talk now?" Max asked.

"It's almost Chloe's bedtime," she said.

"It won't take long," he insisted.

Becca couldn't hold back a sigh. Didn't this man realize how dangerous he was to her with the way he sent her senses spinning and the conflicting emotions he raised in her?

She had no idea what he wanted to discuss, but she didn't really want to stay in the same space with him unless she had to. Even though he seemed different from her impression in Vegas—more well-mannered and attentive—she wondered who the real Max was. And it still irked her that he didn't remember who she was.

But as much as she would have preferred not to spend an extra second with him, she had no choice. She was a guest in his home.

"Lead the way," she said with another sigh.

Hopefully, she would be able to keep her anger at him in check till the conversation was over.

CHAPTER 13

Max watched Becca as she took sips of her coffee. She looked more relaxed than she'd seemed when he'd first met her in the ER. They were seated on the porch at the back of the house. Faint scents of pine and hay drifted in with the cool night breeze. Max passed Becca a blanket, and she wrapped it around her shoulders.

He'd spent some time thinking and praying about this conversation as he'd taken care of Bella earlier in the day, cleaned out her stall, and moved bales of hay. He knew Becca wouldn't have come if not for Chloe, and he wanted to reassure her that he wasn't going to bite or take advantage of her. Though he didn't understand why she felt the way she did about him.

"What did you want to talk about?" Becca asked.

"I know you didn't really want to be here, but I appreciate the fact that you trusted me enough to come," he said.

Becca stayed silent. Max wondered what was going on through her mind.

"And I hope you find your stay here relaxing," he continued. "If you ever need me, I'm usually working around the ranch or in my office beyond the double French doors in the main space, or visiting the sick folks at other ranches."

She looked at him quizzically. "Don't you have to be at Dexington?" she asked. "I thought you worked there."

"No, I only go there once a month," he said, and took a sip of his coffee. "You could also just stop by if you wanted to chat." And why did he feel excitement at that possibility? He wasn't supposed to be looking for anything more than what they had between them.

Max placed his coffee mug by his feet and pulled out a business card from his shirt pocket.

"Here's my phone number. If you don't feel comfortable giving yours to me, please make sure Maggie has it. Given how large this ranch is, it's important for us to know how to reach each other if needed."

"It's not a big deal. I can give you my number." Becca waited till he pulled out his phone, and then she recited her number to him.

Max typed in the digits and froze. What was this? Why was her name and number coming up on his phone? He'd noticed the name Becca in his contacts before, but he'd always figured it belonged to an old colleague or classmate—there were three Beccas in his medical school class—so he'd kept the number instead of deleting it.

Max's heart pounded, and his throat went dry.

"What's wrong?" Becca asked.

He looked up, and his eyes searched her face. "Have we met before?"

CHAPTER 14

Becca's heart thumped at Max's question. "Why do you ask?" she said. She noticed the knuckles that gripped his phone had turned white.

"Why do I have your number already saved on my phone?"

She looked away and stared out into the starry night. She'd forgotten about the possibility that they might have exchanged numbers in Vegas, even though she couldn't recall when.

"Look at me, Becca. I need to know!" he growled out.

How dare he snap at her? She glared back at him.

Suddenly, Max held his head in his hands and groaned.

What was going on? "Max?"

He kept clutching his head and uttered another groan that sent shivers down her spine. Something was wrong here, and she needed to find someone who could help. "I'll be right back," she said.

She got up and raced back into the house and came to a halt where Maggie was watching over Chloe. Chloe was focused on the puzzle she was putting together, and Becca had to be careful not to alarm her.

Maggie looked up and saw Becca's face. "What's wrong?"

"It's Max."

Maggie stood up. "Where is he?" she asked.

"On the porch," Becca said, struggling to keep the panic out of her voice.

"Stay here," Maggie commanded, and hurried off in the direction Becca had come from.

Becca took the seat that Maggie had been in. Her stomach churned, and she kept checking the doorway where Maggie had disappeared. What was wrong with Max, and why was he clutching his head? Was he ill?

Maggie returned after what seemed like a long time and headed straight to the kitchen. Becca got up and followed her there. Maggie grabbed a pitcher of water from the refrigerator and poured herself a glass.

Becca waited for her to finish drinking. "Is he okay?" she asked.

Maggie turned to her. "He's asleep now. He should be better by morning."

"What happened to him?"

Maggie was silent for a moment. "He gets severe headaches any time he's trying to remember something from the past."

Becca's heart beat loudly in her chest. "What do you mean?"

"When he's thinking about something related to his accident."

*B*ecca's heart dropped. "What accident?" she asked Maggie, forcing herself to maintain a steady tone.

"Max was in an accident in Las Vegas five years ago," Maggie said. "And he lost part of his memory in the process, especially what happened around the time of the accident."

Becca's mouth went dry. She'd had no idea. She'd thought he was just pretending to have forgotten her, but he actually had no memory of Vegas and of their time together.

"The doctors say he may or may not recover those memories," Maggie continued in a low voice. "You should have seen him trying so hard to remember them—it was horrific watching him endure those headaches. Then they got so bad that he eventually stopped. My guess is that something important happened in Vegas, but the doctors say it must have been so traumatic for him that his brain closed them off on its own." She poured herself another glass of water and sipped it. "But he hasn't had the headaches for a while now."

"Do you know when the accident happened?" Becca asked.

Maggie thought for a second. "I think it was the morning of May fifth. I remember because it was the ranch manager's birthday, and Max was supposed to be back later that day. We got a call from the hospital since my number was on his phone's speed-dial. Luckily, Dex had just arrived in Vegas so he rushed to be with him, checked his things out from the hotel, and brought him home."

By now Becca's heart was galloping. It was the same day. She'd had no idea. Was the traumatic event what had happened between them?

Maggie peered at her. "Why do you ask?"

Becca pasted a small smile on her face. "I just wanted to know."

"I'm surprised the headaches are back,"

Maggie said. She looked at Becca curiously. "What happened between you two back there on the porch?"

"Nothing really. We were just chatting."

"That's strange." Maggie stared at her for a moment. "Oh dear, you seem to be sweating. Are you okay?"

"I'm fine."

"Alright, don't worry. He'll be fine in the morning."

But all that passed through Becca's mind was that she'd been wrong.

Dead wrong all this time.

CHAPTER 16

*B*ecca put Chloe to bed, but she couldn't sleep. She tossed and turned till she gave up and sat up instead.

How could she have been mistaken? She'd thought Max had blown her off and disappeared. Instead he'd been in an accident.

Wait a second! There had been the accident she'd seen on her way back to the hotel. Could it be …?

She shook her head. No, it wasn't possible. That accident had been so bad that witnesses had speculated the victim was probably dead. It couldn't have been Max, could it?

Her mind raced. The last time she'd seen Max, he'd been calling her name and running after her. And that was when she had crossed the flashing yellow traffic light in her bid to get away from him. Could it be he'd tried to come after her instead of waiting? The light must have turned green by then.

Becca felt a cold dread wash over her.

She had to find out the truth.

And there was only one way to know for sure.

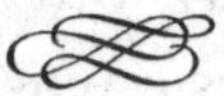

CHAPTER 17

*B*ecca rubbed her gritty eyes. She'd tossed and turned all night and had only fallen asleep a few hours before the alarm she'd set had gone off. She looked at Chloe—the girl was fast asleep. Great.

Becca slipped out of bed, careful not to disturb Chloe, and changed into a T-shirt and a pair of jeans. She expected the morning to still be a bit chilly, so she donned a spring jacket she found in the closet and slipped her feet into a pair of heeled boots. She was sure she looked a mess, but she didn't have time, so she brushed her hair back with her fingers.

She took one look at Chloe and then left the room, closing the door silently behind her. She tiptoed down the stairs. She wasn't sure if Maggie was a light sleeper, and she didn't want to wake her.

The house was quiet and didn't stir when Becca made her way out and headed to the barn. Her best guess was the man she was looking for would be in there feeding the horses. The air was colder than she'd expected, but nothing she couldn't endure. The sky was still somewhat dark, though she knew dawn would come soon.

She entered the large modern rustic-styled timber-framed building and looked around. The interior featured an open concept design with multiple horse stalls, a tack room, and a second-floor hay loft. She walked further into the barn till she saw the man removing manure and wet straw from one of the stalls.

"Hello, Dex," she said.

Dex glanced at her before turning back to the task at hand. "Good morning," he said in a gruff voice.

Okay, so he wasn't exactly enthused about seeing her, but she was a lady on a mission. "Do you have a minute? I need to ask you something."

"I'm listening," he said as he continued mucking out the stall.

Here goes. "Could you tell me more about the accident that Max was in?"

He stilled and looked at her sharply. "Why do you ask?"

"You know why," Becca said softly.

Dex sighed and straightened. "I wasn't sure. You look different from what's on your ID."

"I was younger then. I thought Max had disappeared when I went back to the hotel and found my things with the concierge. Could you tell me what you know?"

Dex looked her straight in the eye, but Becca kept her gaze steady. He must have been satisfied with what he saw, because he leaned the manure fork against the stall wall. "I found him in the hospital—he'd been in an accident. Doctors said witnesses reported he'd been running after someone, but the traffic light changed suddenly, and he got hit. It was only by God's grace that he was alive."

Becca staggered and leaned against a beam to keep from falling. She'd hoped that wasn't the case, but it was true. She'd been the cause of the accident. In her bid to find out what had happened that night between them, she'd only been concerned about herself, and then she'd turned around and blamed him when he wasn't there.

Dex let out another sigh. "He was unconscious when I saw him, but he kept muttering the name Becca. I figured he must have been running after her when he got into the accident. Why didn't you stop?"

"I didn't know," Becca said in a whisper. "I thought he had stopped following me and had returned to the hotel. I only heard about an accident on my way back, and I didn't imagine he could be the victim. I'm so sorry."

"I went back to the hotel, checked out his things, and saw the bag with the ID in it. I dropped anything I guessed wasn't his with the front desk."

And she'd assumed he'd run away when she'd received her things. Instead, she'd been the one that wronged him.

"Listen, I don't know why you guys met up again, but I don't want to see my brother hurt," Dex said. "He's the best man I know, and what you did to him must have hurt him so badly that he doesn't want to remember it. As much as I would prefer you guys handle whatever needs to be resolved between you two, I won't stand by and watch him get hurt again." The conversation was over, because he picked up the manure fork and resumed mucking the stall.

Becca pivoted and left, practically running out the door. This was all too much, and she was finding it hard to breathe. She needed air.

She burst out into the open in front of the barn and placed her hands on her knees as she took big gulps of air. Tears stung at the back of her eyelids as she struggled to get herself under control.

She'd been so wrong. She shouldn't have gone to the restaurant that day—none of this would have happened if she hadn't. She'd been the one who seduced him based on what had been shown on the CCTV, and then she'd hurt him with the accident. It had been all her fault, and yet she'd blamed him all along. What was she going to do now?

Then she noticed she'd stepped on something soft and dark. She looked down. Yikes! Horse dung. How could today get any worse?

"Becca, are you okay?"

Becca looked up to see Max staring down at

her with concern written all over his face. She didn't deserve this kindness. "I'm so sorry," she said in a tremulous voice, and raced toward the mudroom that led into the main house, leaving him standing there.

CHAPTER 18

Max watched as Becca ran into the house. What was wrong, and why did it seem like she'd been crying?

His first instinct was to race after her, but he guessed she needed some privacy. But what had happened? And more importantly, why was she up and about this early in the morning?

His heart squeezed in pain, and he clutched his chest. Now, why was he so affected by just seeing her like this? She was supposed to be a stranger, yet he felt like a part of him had been hurt. But as much as he wanted to go after her, it was probably better to give her some time and then approach her, or better yet, send Maggie to talk to her.

The barn door behind him opened, and he saw Dex step out. "What just happened, Dex?" he asked. "I just saw Becca running into the house in tears."

Dex sighed. "You know I'm not one to poke my head into your matters, Max, and I intend to keep it that way. It's her story to tell," he said.

"What does that mean?"

"Like I said, it's not my place." Dex stepped back into the barn.

Max loved his brother, but he could be so exasperating sometimes. The fear of a repeat of what had happened in the past with Tammy threatened to grip him, but he cast the thought away. He trusted Dex and was certain nothing had happened between him and Becca. And besides, he wasn't in any relationship with her.

But now he was really worried about Becca. What could it be that had caused her to break down like that? Had he done something wrong? And was it related to what had happened last night? He still needed to talk to her about it.

But that could wait. He'd promised her family he'd take care of her, and that he would do.

Even if it meant getting his head bitten off in the process.

$\mathcal{B}$ecca flew into the bathroom and stayed there. Tears threatened to stream down her face, but she held them back. She didn't deserve to cry for what she'd done. She'd accused, misinterpreted, and then almost caused the death of a man she'd taken advantage of. He wouldn't have met her if she hadn't gone to that restaurant with the waiter taking her to his table. And she'd committed one more crime against him which she wasn't ready to face.

She stayed there for the longest time till she heard Chloe waking up. Then she dragged herself out of the bathtub without showering, washed her face, and put on her brightest smile. "Good morning, baby," she said as she stepped out of the bathroom.

"Morning, Mommy!" the most beautiful voice in the world quipped followed by a loud yawn. Then the fresh-faced angel grinned like she'd remembered something. "Can I go and see the horse?" she asked, an impish smile on her face.

Becca managed a chuckle. "After you've brushed your teeth, taken a bath, and eaten breakfast."

"Okay, Mommy," She yawned again. This time, Becca grinned and grabbed her for a morning hug. Chloe accepted it only for like two seconds before she wanted out—she only liked hugs on her terms.

Becca cleaned her up and then took a shower too. She picked out long-sleeved blouses and jeans for Chloe and herself. She didn't know from firsthand experience but had heard that flies and mosquitoes were abundant on farms. There was no sense in giving them more bare skin to perch on than necessary.

They made their way down the stairs for

breakfast. Maggie was already in the kitchen, whipping up some batter.

"Good morning, Maggie," Becca said.

Maggie turned and gave Becca a tired smile. She must not have gotten much rest. "Did you sleep well?" Maggie asked.

"The bed was lovely, thank you," Becca said. She should have been a politician with the way she kept giving vague responses to Maggie's questions. "Anything I can do to help?"

"How about you whisk these and make some scrambled eggs?" Maggie pointed to a small bowl filled with eggs.

"I can do that." She'd learned how to cook once she'd had Chloe.

"Great." Maggie turned to Chloe. "Hello, beautiful," she said to her with a big smile.

Chloe ran up and gave her a hug, which Maggie returned.

"Why don't you sit there, dear?" Maggie said, and gestured at a kid-sized table that hadn't been there yesterday. It was placed far away from the kitchen stove and other electrical appliances for safety reasons yet close enough to maintain enough contact with whoever was in the kitchen. "That's from Max," she said to

Becca. "He put it in this morning for Chloe. Figured she might need it."

Becca didn't know what to say. Here he was trying to make things easier for Chloe, though they still had unresolved issues between them from what had happened yesterday.

A heavy load settled on her heart. She needed to come clean with him, but she just couldn't blurt out the truth that they met in Vegas and she was the cause of his accident. Becca wasn't sure how he would take it. Besides, she'd heard it was better to let people with lost memories recover them on their own—that it was wrong for her to share and influence his memory. Yet, it was going to be hard for her to pretend that all was well.

Breakfast was soon ready, and Max appeared at the table and they settled down to eat. Maggie mentioned that Dex and Jax had grabbed something earlier, since they had a long day ahead of them with spring repairs around the ranch. So it was only Max, Maggie, Becca, and Chloe, seated around the table like a little family. Breakfast was a much simpler feast of blueberry-cinnamon toast, pancakes with maple syrup, scrambled eggs, and cornflake-coated crispy bacon, all washed down with orange juice or coffee.

Becca noticed Max kept stealing glances at her throughout the meal. Had Dex told him about what happened this morning? She didn't think so, otherwise Max would have been mad about it by now.

Or was it because of their unfinished conversation from last night? But no matter what it was, she was glad that he looked alright and seemed to have slept well. She'd been a little scared for him yesterday, despite how angry she'd been with him about everything at the time.

But now that Becca knew she was in the wrong, how was she going to tell him the truth about the biggest secret of all? She kept her eyes down and busied herself with her food. No, she wasn't ready to share it yet. She needed more time. Becca wasn't sure how he would react to the news, but it would definitely affect everything between them. And she wasn't convinced that was what she wanted. She needed time to think it through.

Besides, they were still basically strangers, and she didn't really know much about him.

Maybe that was what she had to do first. Start from a clean slate and learn more about him and then decide the right time to break the news.

Max's voice pulled her out of her reverie. "Becca, this morning looks great for a visit to the horses. What do you think?"

Chloe squealed with joy. She'd been looking forward to this.

So, he hadn't forgotten his promise to Chloe. She appreciated a man of his word. "That's fine," she said. "Maybe in an hour's time when Chloe has had time to digest her food."

Becca watched his ears turn red, and she chuckled. She'd been a greenhorn like him a few years ago, and she was still learning something new every day.

But he recovered quickly. "Okay, ten a.m. it is then," he said.

"But what would she wear?" Becca asked. "She would need a riding habit."

"I believe there's one in the wardrobe. I figured she might need one on the ranch," Maggie said.

They'd thought of everything. It's been so long since she'd had anyone taking care of her needs like they'd done. "Thank you," she said to Maggie with a soft smile.

Max passed her a slip of paper. "Here's the password to the internet. I figured you might need it for your business."

"Thank you." she said and accepted the piece of paper.

"And here's a laptop you can use before yours arrive." He placed a brand-new laptop box at her feet.

"I can't take it," she protested.

"You don't have to. You can just borrow it if you prefer and give it away to someone who might need it after you're done with it. It's up to you."

"This is too much. You've already bought a lot of items for Chloe and me. I know doctors are paid well, but this is a lot of money."

Maggie placed a hand on Becca's arm. "It's nothing. Really."

"Okay. But promise me you won't buy any more stuff for us."

Max chuckled. "That promise is going to be a little hard, but I'll do my best."

His response wasn't perfect, but it had to be enough.

"By the way, your sister also called and said your things would arrive this afternoon," Max said. Now why would Leah call Max instead of reaching out to Becca directly? "She was afraid that they might be able to trace her calls to you."

Oh, she hadn't thought about that. It seemed like a lifetime ago that she'd had the brush with paparazzi. "Thanks for letting me know," she said.

"My pleasure."

Soon, they finished breakfast and moved the plates to the sink.

"I'll take care of the dishes," Max said.

"I'll help," Becca responded.

Maggie brought out coloring paper for Chloe, which she busied herself with at the kiddie table. Then she left them to themselves. She was going into town to spend the day with some friends and would be back in the evening.

Max and Becca washed the dishes in companionable silence. Now that she no longer held any anger against him, Becca observed him out of the corner of her eye. She admired the way his hands made quick work of the dishes. They were callused but spoke of a history of good hard work, and her skin tingled when they accidentally touched hers. His light woodsy peppermint scent enveloped her, and she couldn't help but inhale the fresh scent. It was light, just the way she liked it—she appreciated it when a man didn't douse himself in a whole bottle of perfume.

His nearness made her want to know more about him. Who was Max? "Why did you decide to become a doctor since you love the ranch so much?" she asked.

Max handed her a dish to rinse. "Ma couldn't get the care she needed on time because of how far we were from the city. So I decided to become a doctor so no one in these parts would have to go through what we did. I'm a visiting doctor for the ranches throughout the month except for when I head off to Dexington for my monthly call duty."

"I'm so sorry," Becca said. "I didn't know."

"No worries, it happened a long time ago."

"Have you never thought of living in the city?"

He gave her a small smile. "I'm a country man through and through. I'm used to the city since I went to college and medical school in one, but I prefer the slow pace of life in the countryside."

"But isn't it a lot of work?"

Max passed the last dish to her to rinse. "Everything in life is a lot of work, but it doesn't feel so when it's something you love. What about you? Do you love wedding planning?"

"I've always enjoyed event planning and did so for some celebrity friends, which is how I became popular. And then one of them approached me to plan her wedding, and I had a ton of fun. It turned out I had a strong knack for it, so I planned to pursue it officially as a business."

He glanced at her. "Why didn't you?"

Becca stayed silent and then looked at Chloe.

"I'm sorry," Max said. "I shouldn't have ..."

"I guess we're even now." She placed the rinsed dish on the dish rack.

He chuckled, and the sound turned her inside to mush. "I guess so," he said.

He held her gaze, and she couldn't look away. Becca's heart thumped so loudly she could almost hear it. She was drawn to him by a strong magnetic pull, and she felt herself lean forward.

Max must have felt the same because he moved closer. Their breath intermingled, and Becca felt the butterflies in her stomach begin to rise. Max inched closer. The thought of kissing him made her skin tingle with excitement, and she leaned in more till he was only a breath away.

"I've finished!" Chloe said, and the magic of the moment was broken. Max stepped away and cleared his throat. Becca didn't know what to do with her hands. This was so embarrassing. She'd almost kissed Max just now, and in front of Chloe no less. This was a whole new level of wrong.

She stepped away from the sink and moved toward Chloe. "That's great, baby," she said. Becca took the coloring paper from her and examined it. "This is beautiful."

Chloe beamed and jumped to her feet.

Becca turned to Max. "What do you think?"

He stepped forward and took the proffered paper from Becca. "This is nice, Chloe. Great job." Then he gave her a high-five. Chloe giggled.

Becca guessed she still had about thirty minutes before the horse visit, which gave her enough time to get Chloe changed. She turned to Max. "We need to go and get ready," she said.

Max nodded. "I'll wait for you outside."

Becca left him standing there as she led Chloe upstairs.

But she couldn't forget the kiss that almost happened.

CHAPTER 20

Max watched Becca and Chloe go upstairs. He couldn't believe he'd almost kissed her. It was everything—from how they'd been the only ones at breakfast, giving him that warm cozy family feel he'd always craved, to her nearness as they'd washed the dishes together.

What had he been thinking? He was supposed to keep her safe, not take advantage of her. But he couldn't forget the way he'd almost drowned in her beautiful green eyes and how her lips had beckoned to him. It was a good thing Chloe had been there to bring them back to reality. He would have to be more careful.

Becca had seemed okay at breakfast,

compared to how she'd been earlier this morning. He hoped that meant whatever was bothering her had been resolved. But he still needed to talk to her about last night.

Why did he have her number saved on his phone? He couldn't remember meeting her before, and the only gap in his memory was the time around the accident … which meant he probably met her around that time too.

If she was in Vegas, what had happened between them? Had they just met randomly there and he got her number, or had there been something else? And why were his headaches associated with her? It was a mystery he was keen on solving, and she could help him unravel the case.

Maybe their horse visit with Chloe was a good time to bring it up. He'd noticed Becca was most relaxed when around her. Yes, he would try and bring it up today.

But first he had to pick something up. He strode to the mudroom and put on his worn boots and a hat. Then he brought out a small package he'd kept in one of the baskets. He'd promised Becca no more gifts, but he'd bought these items before that agreement, so it didn't count in this case.

He was ready for the visit, and he hoped she was too.

It was the only way he could get the answers he needed.

CHAPTER 21

Max waited outside for Becca and Chloe. The weather was perfect for a ride—cool but not chilly. He planned to introduce Chloe to Bella and then teach her how to feed her some treats. He would love to have her ride Rusty, his quarterhorse pony, since he was good with children, and he'd prepped him just in case. But it was baby steps with this one.

Becca and Chloe stepped out looking fantastic in their riding habits. Becca looked stunning, her outfit hugging her in the right places. He loved a woman with soft curves, and Becca had them in spades. Truth be told, it was going to be tough looking elsewhere, when all he wanted to do was feast on her with his eyes.

Max stepped forward. "You look great," he said.

Becca blushed. Oh my, he had no idea he would get that kind of reaction from her. She'd always been cool with him except this morning, so it was interesting to see this other side of her.

What had changed? He had no idea, but he liked it a lot. Today was bound to be interesting. Who knew what else she would show him?

He reached out and lifted Chloe into his arms. "Time to go visit the horse," he said.

"Yay!" Chloe screamed and almost knocked her helmet askew. Max adjusted it to make sure it was secure.

They soon reached the barn and stopped at the entrance. Max put Chloe down and then knelt to her eye level. "Chloe, there are some rules you must obey."

Chloe scrunched up her face. "Rules?"

"Yes, so that you and Bella will be safe. Can you do that for me?"

"Okay."

"Horses are very big, but you don't have to be afraid."

"Okay."

"They can hurt us without knowing because they are big."

"Okay."

"So no running or screaming."

"Why?"

"So you don't scare them."

"Horses get scared?"

"All the time. They are big babies."

"Okay. No running," Chloe said.

"Or screaming. And never stand at her back."

She nodded. "Can we go and see Bella now?"

"One more thing. You must obey what I tell you."

"Why?"

"Because I want you to be safe."

"Okay." She hopped from one leg to the other.

"So what did I say?"

"Horses are big and scary babies. No running. No standing at the back."

"No screaming, and you must listen to me."

"Okay."

"Let's go." He lifted her up and then carried her into the barn.

Bella's stall was at the back, so they headed in that direction. Chloe's eyes were round and big as she took in each horse they passed. When they reached Bella's stall, Max handed off Chloe to Becca. "Give me one second," he said. He walked further and picked up a small bench he kept in the corner. He placed it close to the door of Bella's stall and then stood Chloe on it. "She'll be able to see and touch Bella better."

"Is Bella high strung?" Becca asked.

"Not really."

By now, Bella had gotten up from where she lay and walked to the door of the stall at the sound of his voice. She nuzzled her nose into the back of his shirt. Chloe giggled.

Max turned and gave Bella a pat on the neck. "Bella, I have a new friend called Chloe. Do you want to say hi?"

Bella neighed.

Max brought out a small apple and handed it to Chloe. "Put it flat on your hand." She did. "Okay offer it to her. Slowly, slowly." Chloe offered the apple to Bella who took it and chomped it down. "Good girl. Now put out your hand and rub her side like this." He showed her how to do it. "Very nice. Now touch her neck like this." Chloe did the same. "She seems to like it. See how she is coming closer?" Chloe rubbed her some more. "Good job, Chloe."

"She is soft like Fluffy," Chloe stated.

Max gave Becca a questioning look. "Who is Fluffy?"

Becca chuckled. "Her favorite monkey."

Oh. "Where is this said monkey?"

"Back in Dexington. He might come with my luggage."

"Okay, I'm thinking of saddling Bella and having Chloe ride with me along the trail," Max said.

"Can I be on the horse instead?"

"Can you ride?"

"Yes."

Max eyed her. He wasn't sure if she was being serious. But he'd give her the benefit of the doubt, though he planned to lead her by the rope just in case.

Max handed Chloe back to Becca and then walked over to the tack room and picked up what he needed. He saddled Bella up and then walked her out of the barn. Becca followed him a short distance away to the side.

He stopped when he was outside a fenced area and then offered the reins to Becca. "Since you can ride a horse, I'm sure you can mount her easily as well."

Becca laughed. "Is that a challenge?"

Max's lips twitched into a smile. "Would you like it to be?"

"How about you skip dessert if I win?"

"And if you lose?"

"What do you want?"

"A kiss." Did he just say that out loud? Yep, he did—Becca was blushing. *What's wrong with you, Max?* he thought. "Sorry, I wasn't thinking."

"Of course, you weren't. But since it's what you want, I'll grant it to you if I lose. Because I won't."

"Deal."

"Buckle down, cowboy. Here I come."

Max chuckled. This he had to see.

Becca handed Chloe to Max and then took the reins.

She spoke softly to Bella. "Good girl," he overheard her say.

And then before he could say Jack Robinson, Becca put her left leg in the stirrup, mounted Bella in one swift motion, and stayed up there like the saddle was home. Bella didn't budge.

"Hey, you didn't tell me you were a pro," he called out.

"You didn't ask." Becca took off, riding Bella in a canter twice around the fenced area before she slowed to a stop.

"Where did you learn to ride like that?" Max asked.

"I used to play polo."

Max's eyes widened. "Are you serious?"

"Serious as a heart attack."

"Hey, don't joke about stuff like that. At our age, it's more common than you think."

Becca chuckled. "Sorry, I couldn't help it."

"So should I hand Chloe to you?"

"You better or she's going to talk your ear off tonight."

"That's not so bad."

"Wait till you experience it. Then you can let me know whether you like it or not."

"Okay, here you go." He lifted Chloe and plopped her in front of Becca. He watched Becca teach her how to relax into the mount and hold the reins and then they were off on a walk around the fenced area.

Max leaned against the fence and watched them go—mother and daughter duo looking great in their outfits. He loved seeing them together.

When they got back, Chloe said, "Again, Mommy." So they went another round.

By now, the sun had really come out, and Max figured it was enough for one day for Chloe. This was her first time horse riding, and it was better for her to get used to it slowly.

When they arrived back, Becca handed Chloe to him. "I think I need to go one more time." She took off in a gallop, her ponytail flying high behind her. She ended up going around the fenced area three times and then walked the horse for one more time before coming to a stop. "That was fun," she said. "I've missed this." Then she dismounted and led Bella to the shaded area behind the barn. Max watched as Becca removed the tack and then cooled the horse down. She hugged Bella when she was done, and Bella neighed in response.

"I think you've made a new friend," Max said.

"I sure have. I think she's dry now."

"Okay, let's take her back to her stall."

Once Bella was safely ensconced, Max added extra hay to her stall and then made sure the other horses were safe. He walked back to the tack room and then picked up the gift from where he had stashed it.

"Here you go," he said and handed the package to Becca.

"What is this?"

"Open it and see."

"I thought we agreed no more gifts."

"I'd already bought it before then."

"Alright, but this is the last one."

Becca opened the package and pulled out the items. Chloe squealed in delight. They were matching cowboy hats in deep burgundy— Chloe's had pink flowers bordering the base. Becca removed their helmets and plopped the hats on their heads.

"Now you are cowgirls." Max said.

Becca posed. "You think?"

Max laughed. He was enjoying hanging out with these two.

He reached out and lifted Chloe into his arms. "Time to go back to the house," he said. "Would you like a glass of orange juice?"

"Yes!" Chloe screamed and almost knocked

her hat off. Max caught it in time and placed it back firmly on her head.

As they walked back to the house, the sound of tires crunching on the driveway reached his ears before the SUV appeared and then stopped in front of the house.

He peered at the passengers from where he stood. Who could they be, and what were they doing here? Then he recognized Jasmine, and his shoulders relaxed. He knew without looking further who the other two were. He'd planned to ask Becca about last night once Chloe was occupied with her juice, but that was a moot point at this time. The arrival of the ladies had changed everything.

"I can't believe this," Becca said from beside him.

The Terrific Trio had arrived.

CHAPTER 22

"*A*unt Becca, this area is so pretty. Have you thought about using it for weddings?" Jasmine asked as she, Alicia, and Dana lounged on the massive couch in the living room. All three were roommates and best friends that lived in an apartment they'd rented from Becca.

"You speak as if I live here." Becca brushed away Chloe's hair from her face as she lay napping beside Becca.

"You could always come to an agreement with Max," Jasmine countered. Max had disappeared into his office once he'd welcomed them. Becca had a feeling he would hide out there till the ladies were gone.

Becca shook her head in disbelief. That wasn't going to be possible. And Max liked his privacy from what she had seen. "So what are you ladies doing here?"

"Well, we came to relax and discuss wedding plans per Blake's suggestion," Alicia said. Alicia, Blake's fiancée, was a third-year internal medicine resident.

"Wasn't that suggestion just made *yesterday*?"

"We're pretty quick on the uptake," Jasmine said as she took a sip of the iced lemonade that Becca had offered her.

"Can we just be real here? We're excited about planning our wedding together, and once we realized we were all free this weekend, we hopped into the car and came right away," Dana said. Dana was a fourth-year general surgical resident and was engaged to Josh Roman, Blake's best friend.

"Or don't you like that we are here? Are we disturbing some *special goings-on* with a certain *doctor*?" Jasmine teased.

"Ooh!" Alicia and Dana echoed.

"I've seen the way the good doctor looks at you," Jasmine said.

Alicia leaned forward. "Have you kissed?" she asked.

"Is he a good kisser?" Dana piled on.

Becca lifted her hands in surrender. "I can't even ..." She lowered her voice. "He can hear you!"

"Isn't that good? That way he can get the ball rolling if he hasn't," Jasmine said.

"You girls are crazy!"

"And we love you too, Aunt Becca," Alicia said.

"Why does the way you say my name make me sound old?" Becca said.

"You? Old? No way. You're just a spring chicken," Jasmine said with a smirk.

Becca threw a pillow from the couch at her head. Jasmine ducked and laughed.

"Ooh, what's that?" Alicia got up and made her way to the mantel over the fireplace. Becca looked in her direction to see what had caught her attention. Alicia picked up a framed photo. "This picture looks familiar, like I've seen it before."

"Really? Let me see," Becca said. Alicia brought over the picture. It was a black and white photo of a group of people standing in front of a wagon. "I asked Max about it," she said. "It's a picture of his ancestors with their relatives when they first arrived in America." Jasmine and Dana rushed over to see what they were referring to.

"I'm serious. I've seen this exact photo, though I can't remember where," Alicia insisted.

"That's interesting," Becca said. "Maybe it will come to you some other time."

"I know this picture," Jasmine said. "I've seen it too."

The others turned eager faces at her. "Where?" Alicia asked.

"In your dreams, ha ha!" Jasmine said.

Alicia grabbed her in a headlock. "I think you need to be taught a lesson," Alicia said. "What do you think, Dana?"

"Yep," Dana said with a serious face. "Some major tickling is in order." Dana pounced on Jasmine, and they all collapsed in a heap, with Jasmine alternating between flailing, laughing, and begging, while Alicia and Dana chuckled.

"I'm sorry, I'm sorry," Jasmine pleaded.

"Okay, we'll let you off for now," Alicia said.

"As long as you behave," Dana added.

Becca leaned back. These crazy girls. She

loved them like little sisters. And she knew they had come down to cheer her up after what happened with the paparazzi. "Settle down, ladies."

Dana, Jasmine, and Alicia returned to the couch.

"So let's talk about the wedding," Becca continued. "The planning would be so much easier if they were all happening on the same day," she muttered to herself. Becca noticed them exchange looks. "What?" She looked from Alicia to Dana to Jasmine. "Hold on for a second. You can't really—"

"That's a great idea," Alicia said. "What do you think, girls?"

"It would save me the stress," Dana said.

"It would be so rad," Jasmine said.

She'd only been joking. "Ladies, that's not going to happen, hello!"

"Why not?" Alicia asked.

"Aren't Jasmine and Dana supposed to be your maids of honor?" Becca said.

Alicia's face fell. "True. That's a bummer."

"But what if we have the weddings one after the other?" Jasmine asked. "We change into each other's bridesmaid dresses once we're needed."

Becca shook her head. "The logistics would be a nightmare," she said.

Dana crossed her legs. "How about we have the weddings over three days, one for each of us? We'll still all have our special days, and we don't have to worry about changing in and out of the bridesmaids dresses."

Alicia raised an eyebrow. "Can you imagine Blake marrying me and waiting a day or two before going on honeymoon? I can tell you that's so not happening." They all chuckled at the thought.

"Yes, that would be tricky," Dana said.

But it seemed Jasmine hadn't given up. "How about we marry in the morning, afternoon, and evening? We each get our special time and be each other's bridesmaids and have enough time to change into the outfits. The honeymoon doesn't have to be delayed, since it's on the same day," she suggested.

"That would be perfect," Alicia and Dana echoed.

"But we'll have to move it back a little," Jasmine said. Jasmine had had a double mastectomy for breast cancer, and was still recovering from the surgery. "I need to be more healed up before I walk down the aisle."

"We can do that," Alicia said.

"But what about your invitation cards?" Dana asked. "I thought those had gone out."

"No, they haven't. We'll need new ones anyway, since the cards have to list all three weddings on them."

"But we haven't told the guys though," Dana said. "I wouldn't want us to get all excited and then be let down."

"Do you really think they can resist *all three of us*?" Jasmine said with a twinkle in her eyes.

"Okay, next!" Alicia said.

They burst into laughter. Becca watched them with a smile on her face. She remembered when she was young and fresh-faced like this. Those had been the glory days. But still she was grateful for this season in her life—older and sometimes wiser with a beautiful kid to boot. She really was doing great.

But it was time to corral these ladies before they developed other harebrained ideas. "Okay, let's start from the top," she said.

Sunday morning dawned bright and early. Jasmine, Alicia, and Dana had spent the rest of the day with Becca, their time together filled with lots of planning and laughter. Jasmine had also brought Becca's things, which was wonderful.

But she'd also delivered the news that the paparazzi were still hovering with no change in sight, so Becca might have to spend time at the ranch longer than she'd planned. She'd mentioned it to Max when he emerged from his cave, but he hadn't seemed to mind. Blake had sent a driver to bring the trio back, and they'd left after promising to come again soon. It had been a good day, but Becca was happy to retire early and had gotten a good rest.

Max had asked her last night if she would like to go to church with them, and Becca had agreed. They'd had a light breakfast, and she stood before the mirror now in a deep purple coat dress that was a favorite of hers. Chloe wore a miniature version in royal blue.

Becca picked up her purse and a small Bible she kept by her side, then held Chloe's hand, and walked down the stairs. Max waited at the bottom of the stairs in a light blue dress shirt tucked into dark jeans and paired with dark brown boots. He looked spiffy, if she said so herself.

"You look beautiful," he said in that voice that turned her insides to mush.

That faint Western drawl. The guy had no idea what his voice did to her. Becca gave him a shy smile in return.

Max turned to Chloe. "And you, my princess, look very nice."

"Like a princess?" Chloe asked.

"Yes, like a princess."

Chloe giggled. Max took her hand and gave the back a kiss, and Chloe giggled some more.

He lifted her up into his arms and led the way out of the house. Parked in front was a dark blue Lamborghini Urus instead of the truck Max liked to drive.

Becca looked at Max in surprise. She recognized the car from a car show she'd attended, and it was very expensive. How could Max afford it on a doctor's salary, especially since he didn't work full time? Was the ranch bringing in that much money? As much as Becca loved expensive things, she believed in only spending what one could afford. Maybe she could talk to Max about it one of these days.

Max had already transferred the car seat from his truck to the car, and he secured Chloe safely in it. Becca walked over to the other back passenger door, but Max's voice stopped her. "Becca, would you mind sitting in the front?"

She turned to look at him, and he already held the front passenger door open for her. She hesitated for a moment and then headed to where he stood and sat in the front seat. Before she knew it, Max had secured the seatbelt for her as well.

It wasn't supposed to be a big deal, but somehow Becca felt there was a shift in the air with this simple action. Like their relationship had gone from being casual acquaintances to something much more.

Max looped around to the driver's seat and slid in. He turned the ignition on, and then they were on their way.

The ride to church was generally quiet, though she noticed Max kept glancing at her. When she couldn't stand it any longer, she had to ask. "Do I have something on my face?" she said.

The corners of his lips twitched into a smile. "Becca, I'd like to court you if that's okay with you."

Becca released an involuntary cough. How could he ask her out, just like that, on their way to church?

"Are you alright?" he asked, his voice full of concern.

"I'm fine. Just reeling from this sudden *confession*," she said.

"You don't want to date me?"

"It's not that."

"So, you do want to go out with me?"

Becca threw up her hands in the air. "I give up!"

Max burst into a hearty laughter that warmed her soul. 'So what do you say, Becca?"

A mischievous smile hovered over Becca's lips. "We'll see."

"Is that a challenge?"

"You think?"

Max kept smiling, and Becca's heart sang. But then she remembered the decision she still had to make, and her smile faded.

Max continued stealing glances at her.

"What is it this time?" she asked.

"You're just really beautiful, that's all."

Becca's face warmed. "Thank you," she managed to say.

The rest of the drive went quickly, and soon they'd arrived at their destination—a quaint mid-century stone church with a lovely red barn door and a tall steeple. Max stepped out and then opened the door for Becca before lifting Chloe from the backseat.

Then he held out a hand to her. "Do you mind?"

Becca looked from the proffered hand to Max's face. Max wanted to hold her hand and enter church. This was a big deal. He really meant this business about wooing her! Even though she almost turned him down, a part of her wanted to enjoy the moment. So she slipped her hand into his, and he held her firmly and led her into the church, slowing his pace to match hers.

Curious eyes stared at them as Max led her to his family pew. He sat down on one end with Chloe between them. Only then did he release her hand, and she felt the loss immediately. Jax and Dex joined them, and if Dex noticed anything different between them, he said nothing.

The service went by pretty fast, and soon it was over. Jax and Dex left immediately to head back to the ranch. Max picked up Chloe, who had fallen asleep and then slipped his hand over Becca's. He exchanged pleasantries with some friendly folk who had stepped up to greet him and introduced her as his friend. It was as if he'd read her mind that it was what she preferred for now. A fellow rancher called Max's name, and he stepped away for a minute to talk with him.

"You are not his first you know." Becca turned to see a willowy young woman standing next to her in a flowery dress. But her penetrating gaze was what put Becca on high alert.

Becca thought for a moment. Of course that was expected. She would be more concerned if he hadn't had anyone in his life before, considering his age. She saw Max turn and smile at her before returning back to his conversation.

"His first girlfriend and longtime sweetheart jilted him at the altar. You might want to stay clear."

Becca's hackles rose. Who was this strange woman, and why was she butting into Becca's business? And for some reason, the woman looked familiar, though Becca couldn't place where she'd met her. She hated people like this who loved to smear and tarnish other people's reputations.

Becca put on her sweetest smile. "Bless your heart," she said and walked off to where Max stood. He'd just finished the conversation with the ranchers who were now on their way. She slipped her hand into his, and he held hers as if it was the most natural thing in the world.

"Would you like to visit the town?" Max asked.

"Truthfully? I'd like to just go back to the ranch."

"I didn't know you were a hermit."

"You've rubbed off on me."

Max chuckled. "Okay, how about we grab something to go?"

"That would be perfect."

They walked back to where they'd parked, and Max opened the door for her, before settling Chloe in her car seat. He closed her door when she was done and then turned around and entered the car.

Becca felt eyes on her and turned her head to see the woman who had spoken to her earlier standing and watching her with a black expression as they drove off. The hairs on Becca's neck rose, and she shivered. Something about the woman was off, and she hoped she never saw her again.

They drove into town and parked on the street in front of a bustling restaurant. The curtains were open, and the place was teeming with people.

"This place must be super popular," Becca said.

"Yes. Most folks drop by here on Sundays. What would you like me to get you? I know you'd prefer to stay in the car rather than have us disturb Chloe's nap."

Becca looked at him in surprise. "How did you know? Are you a mind reader?"

"I wish I was—I would know all your secrets." He winked at her.

Becca laughed. "Oh, just go. I'll take whatever you'll have."

"Coming right up."

Max got out and entered the restaurant. Becca watched the people coming and going on the street. The place reminded her of a miniature version of Newbury street in Boston, and she hoped she'd have another chance to explore the place.

Max stepped out, sooner than she'd expected, holding two huge shopping bags. A woman with silvery hair cut into a short bob followed behind him.

Max gestured for Becca to lower her window which she did. "Becca, I'd like to introduce you to Miss Prissy, Maggie's old friend."

"How do you do, ma'am?" Becca said.

Kind eyes smiled at her. "Oh, please, Miss Prissy would do just fine," she said. "Max, you've got a good one here. You take good care of her, you hear?"

"Yes, ma'am."

"Becca, it's good to meet you. I hope we get a chance to chat some other time. I have to go before Joe burns down the building. Joe is my husband," she said with a twinkle in her eye. "Oh my, I didn't even see the little one in the back. Max, she looks so much like your mom did when we were just little girls. Anyway, see you soon. Bye!" She strode off before Becca could get in a word.

Max laughed. "That's Miss Prissy for you. She spied you in the car and insisted on coming out to meet you. She's one of the best cooks in town, but also its biggest source of gossip. She knows almost everything you want to know about anyone that lives in this town. I have a feeling people come here more for the gossip than for the food!"

"Aren't you worried?"

"About what?"

"That the news you're hanging out with a single mom will join the rumor mill."

Max chuckled. "I don't care about any of that. And for your information, I enjoy hanging out with a *certain* single mom. In fact, I would love to kiss that woman now."

Becca began to raise the window. "You are

crazy." She was sure her cheeks were red like a tomato.

Max laughed and then turned around the car and dropped the bags into the footwell of the backseat before sliding into the driver's seat.

The conversation flowed easily between them as they drove back to the ranch. Becca found herself laughing and smiling more. She had no idea Max was so funny and such a big tease. She wished the conversation would go on and on and was sad when they drew up in front of the house.

"How about we go to the movies?" Max asked.

"We just came back from town," Becca reminded him.

"We have a movie theatre in the house. I was thinking we could hang out there."

"Really? I had no idea."

"It's in the basement."

"You have a lot of modern amenities for a cowboy, cowboy."

Max shrugged. "Nothing wrong with having things that make your life easier. So what do you say?"

"Is there going to be popcorn?"

"If you like."

"Deal."

Max helped Becca out of the car and then picked up Chloe, who had woken up. "You awake, princess?" he asked.

"Yes." Chloe yawned. Becca and Max chuckled.

"I'm hungry, Mommy," Chloe said.

"Don't worry we are going to eat now once we get you changed, okay?"

Chloe nodded.

They were changed and down to eat in record time. And the meal was delicious. Maggie joined them—she'd been feeling tired but was now better. After the dishes were done, Max rummaged through the pantry till he found what he was looking for.

"What are you doing in my kitchen, Max?" Maggie asked.

Max turned around with a look like he'd been found with his hand in the cookie jar. "I need to make popcorn."

Maggie looked from Becca to Max. "Why don't you two head down? Chloe and I will make the popcorn and bring it to you."

closed her eyes again and snuggled in further into his arms. This was nice. She loved the feel of his arms around her, solid and dependable. And she felt safe. She could sense her heart thawing as she spent more time with him.

She'd never thought she'd meet Max again, find out the truth, and then fall for him. Because that was what had happened. She had fallen for Max. And her heart had always known what her mind was only realizing.

But it wasn't enough. She had a child, and it was more important than ever that she made the right decision. Becca was a city girl, though she'd come to crave the solitude the country life provided. She could see herself spending her life here. But Max had made it clear he was a country man. Would he ever be open to spending some time in the city?

And then she was concerned about his money situation. He seemed to spend a lot, and she was worried that one day he would end up in debt that could ruin them both.

But most of all, she wanted to start off her wedding planning business, and she wasn't sure how that would fit into living in the valley. And finally, there was the big lie that stood between them, that had the potential to change everything. She still hadn't decided on what to do about it.

She looked up at his face and studied the long eyelashes that graced his eyelids. She was tempted to trace her finger down the curve of his nose, but she held herself back.

And then his eyelids opened, and intense blue eyes stared back at her. She wanted to pull away, but it was as if they kept her rooted in the spot.

Her eyes flashed briefly to his lips. And Becca knew at that moment that she wanted to kiss him.

Max lifted his hand and traced the curve of her face. Her breath quickened at his feathery touch, and the butterflies in her stomach came alive. She couldn't help but lean into the feel of his hand against her face. He leaned forward, his breath fanning her face and his woodsy peppermint scent enveloping her, which sent the butterflies in her tummy into overdrive. His eyes searched hers, and after a moment's hesitation, Max bent his head and kissed her.

The kiss was light, gentle, telling her she was treasured, and causing her nerve endings to sizzle. It was everything and more than she'd imagined. Yet she wanted more.

She leaned forward and looped her hands around his neck. That was all the permission Max needed, because he deepened the kiss, driving away all her doubt and hesitation, and assuring her he was here to stay. She burrowed deeper into his arms, wanting to be nowhere else but with him. They kissed for a while, the experience both heartwarming and exhilarating.

Then she spotted something in his hair, and she broke away laughing.

"What so funny?" he asked.

"Nothing," she said as she hid a smile. She was going to enjoy this joke on him, and it was not her place to interfere. "I think it's time we returned to humanity."

"Can't we just stay like this a little bit longer, you in my arms?"

"Okay, but no kissing."

"That's tough, but possible."

"Thank you, cowboy."

They stayed that way for a while. The silence felt comfortable, cozy even.

Then Max said, "Becca, there's something I need to tell you."

Becca sat up. "What is it?"

Max chuckled. "Relax, lady. There's no need to be scared. Just something you need to know about me."

"What is it?"

"I have a lot of money."

"Like—"

"A lot. Much more money than I could ever spend in a lifetime. I got some inheritance with my mom's passing and invested the money into some young technology startups on the advice of my roommate and best friend in college at the time, who was into all things stock. The investments paid off, and I ended up with a lot of money, much more than you can imagine. He still manages my investments today."

"Oh." It surprised her that the fact that he was probably a billionaire didn't turn her off him like it normally would.

"Is that all you have to say?"

"I'm just relieved. I was worried you were spending all this money you didn't have."

Max laughed. "I just enjoy spending it on you and Chloe. I'm otherwise conservative by nature. Sometimes, I feel like I'm only a steward of the money, and all I need to do is make sure I spend it on the things that matter."

"That makes total sense, considering it's the Lord who gives us wealth."

"I agree. And I'm glad to have eliminated that concern of yours."

"You're welcome. Since you've told me your secret, I'll tell you mine."

"What is it?"

"I don't really need to work. I have millions stashed away in bank accounts both from my inheritance and from my previous event planning gigs, which paid a lot. Even though I was a celebrity, my daily needs were simple. Well except for my high heels—you would have to pry them away from my cold hands."

"Duly noted. Thanks for telling me."

"Now, let's cuddle some more before we go get Chloe."

Max blessed the food, and everyone bent their heads and began to eat. Today had been great, from the service, to lunch, and finally to the special time he'd spent with Becca. He couldn't believe she'd agreed to go out with him. He'd been thinking about it and decided to just go for it. And it had been worth it. He looked forward to spending more time with her and getting to know her more.

Then he noticed that every minute or so, someone at the table would chuckle or giggle. It happened so often, that he eventually placed his fork down. "What is it?" he asked.

No one answered. Everyone seemed intent

"Thanks, Maggie. You are a dear." He gave her a kiss on the cheek.

"Oh. Go on," she said, though she was as pleased as could be.

Max led Becca to the basement. The movie theatre was huge with large brown seats that were super comfortable. "What would you like to watch?" Max asked.

"I don't know. I watch everything except horror. What about you?"

"I love anything with drama or suspense in them. But I'm open to whatever you want."

"How about a comedy flick?"

Max laughed. "Coming right up."

He found the disc he was looking for, inserted it, and soon the image filled the room.

They settled in next to each other to watch.

Becca opened her eyes to see that they were still in the movie theatre. Her head rested against Max's chest and his arm looped around her, holding her close.

She smiled and then yawned. They'd both fallen asleep in the middle of the movie. She

on moving their forks from the plates in front of them to their mouths.

Max picked up his fork again, and then he heard another chuckle. "That's it. You have to tell me what is going on or this dinner stops right here."

Everyone at the table burst out in laughter.

"That was so hard to hold in," Jax said.

"Me too," Maggie echoed.

What was going on? What were they talking about? Maybe he should ask Dex, the sensible one.

But Dex had a big grin on his face.

"Can someone put him out of his misery?" Maggie said as she chuckled. "Becca?"

"Becca dear, could you tell me what's going on?" Max asked and took a sip of water.

"Dear? Did I miss something?" Jax said as he looked from Max to Becca.

"Mommy and Max were sleeping together!" Chloe announced.

Max almost spat out the drink in his mouth. Becca was staring at Chloe in shock.

"Wait! What?" Dex looked at Max in confusion.

"They slept together in the theatre while watching a movie, right, Chloe?" Maggie asked.

"Yes."

Max could see the look of relief on the faces around the table.

"Oh, that's what she means," Jax said.

"Wait, hold on," Max said. "But that's not what you guys were laughing about."

"Max, dearest," Becca said. "You have this tiny little thing on your hair."

"My hair? Where?"

"Say cheese." And a camera clicked. It was Jax taking a picture on his phone. "I need ammunition for the day you give me a hard time."

Max rang a hand through his hair, removing the colorful hair tie that had turned a small section of the top of his hair into a spiky mini-ponytail. Then he reached out for Jax's phone. "Give me that."

"No way. I need something to threaten you with when required."

Max got up from the table. "Jax, give it to me while I'm being nice."

Jax jumped up as well. "Nope. Sorry, old dude."

"Boys, settle down!" Maggie said in her no-nonsense voice.

Max sat down grudgingly, and Jax followed suit.

"Max, the head tie was a special gift from Chloe. What do you do when somebody does something nice for you?"

Max turned to Chloe. "Thank you, Chloe."

Chloe beamed. "You're welcome." Max heard a couple snickers, and he glowered at Jax.

"Now, Jax, let me have your phone," Maggie said.

"Can't I keep it?"

"No, you can't. Hand it over."

Jax passed the phone reluctantly to Maggie. Maggie fiddled with it. "There. Deleted."

"Thanks, Maggie," Max said.

A phone beeped. Everyone looked in Maggie's direction. She picked up her phone and opened the screen. Then she looked up and flashed the screen at him. "Sorry, Max, I had to keep a copy."

Jax fell over himself with laughter. "Max, welcome to toddlerhood."

"Let's just eat," Maggie said, though she was grinning from ear to ear.

It occurred to Max that this was going to be his new life—filled with unimaginable toddler antics.

And guess what?

He didn't mind at all.

CHAPTER 26

Becca stretched and closed her laptop. It had been a fruitful morning. She'd worked on compiling the lists of detailed wedding plans that would ensure the triple wedding went off without a hitch. She'd realized a boatload of work needed to be done, so she'd called up her old assistant, who was more than happy to join her in this new venture. She was scheduled to start work next week.

Becca had also reached out to vendors she'd worked with in the past whom she trusted. They'd been happy to hear from her and looked forward to working with her again. But best of all, she'd seen a glimpse of how possible it was for her to run her business from here. So her morning had been productive. Now she had the rest of the day to spend with Max and Chloe.

She got up and stretched. Memories of yesterday filled her mind, especially the kisses. She'd even rewarded Max with another one, when no one was looking, for handling the Chloe embarrassment like a champ. The kisses had been heavenly, glorious, with a thousand other words she could use to describe them.

But most of all, she was at peace with herself and knew today was the day to tell him the secret.

A knock sounded on her door. "Come in," she said.

The door opened, and Max filled the entrance. "What are you up to?" he asked.

"Just taking care of some wedding planning stuff."

Max leaned against the door frame. "Is the work easy for you to handle from here?"

"About sixty percent of it," Becca replied. "Forty percent would have to be done in person. So I'm trying to take care of the sixty percent first."

"Sounds like a good strategy."

Becca nodded. "Do you need anything from me?"

Max wriggled his eyebrows. "Kisses?"

Becca laughed. "You wish. Max, be serious!"

"Alright, alright. Would you like to go on a picnic with me?"

Max led Becca as they rode their horses down the trail till they arrived at the picnic area he'd selected. Chloe had gone with Maggie to buy groceries and was as happy as a clam to do so. So Max and Becca had a few hours together before Chloe would be back, and the weather was nice and perfect for some outdoor time.

Soon they reached the giant oak tree that had been there since the ranch was established many generations ago. Max mentioned he loved to come here when he needed some peace and quiet.

He dismounted, and Becca followed suit.

Max spread the blanket he had packed and placed the picnic basket on it. Then he released the horses to graze in a nearby field.

"Welcome to Dexin Oak," he said with a wave of his hand.

"Thank you, good sir," Becca responded and sat on the blanket. "This is a huge tree," she said as she patted its trunk.

Max plopped down too. "It's been here for many generations. It gets enough nutrients from its location, so I imagine it living on for many more years. It's constant and unmoving, and that's why I love it."

"It reminds me of God," Becca said.

"Right? Steadfast and unmoving."

He began to unpack the food that Maggie had put together. There was buttermilk chicken, potato salad, corn bread, fresh fruits, and iced tea. Becca filled each plate with food from each dish and handed one of the plates to Max. They leaned against the tree, enjoying the food, good conversation, and a wonderful breeze. And when they finished, Max read a little from a poetry book he'd found many years ago among his mother's things. Becca closed her eyes and enjoyed the rise and fall of his voice mingling with the sounds of nature.

"Becca, I was engaged before."

Becca's eyes flew open, and she sat up. This was probably what that weird woman from church was talking about.

"She was my high school sweetheart, and we went out all through college and medical school," Max said. "And when I finally proposed, she seemed really happy. We planned our wedding and everything. There was no hint or sign that something was amiss. Then on the day of the wedding, I waited for her till I realized she was never coming. First, I thought she was just late, then I imagined one and a million things had happened to her, and then I finally got the note that she had skipped town with a ranch hand and didn't want to be bound forever to this valley.

"Of course, I didn't believe it was true. She'd never hinted that she hated the town or wanted to live in the city. And then the rumors started flying around that she'd left with my brother."

"Brother?" Was he talking about the one that wasn't around? Because Dex and Jax were as loyal as they come.

"My brother, Rex. He's Jax's twin. He'd always had a crush on Tammy—that was her name—but I never thought anything would come of it. I didn't want to believe it, and I still don't now, but Rex disappeared the same day she did and has never come back. Jax gets the occasional phone call from him, so we know he is okay, but we never talk about it. He doesn't answer my phone calls and has made no attempt to reach out to me. Sometimes, I wish he would just come home and tell me to my face what happened. And I miss him. He was funny, loud, though a bit bull-headed, and he had his heart in the right place.

"I was so devastated by what happened that I couldn't function for weeks. Jax finally shipped me off to Vegas for a national rodeo event, and then I had the accident."

"I'm so sorry."

"You shouldn't be. I just wanted you to know that about me and not hear it from anyone else."

"Thank you for letting me know. It sucks being left out in the cold just like that. I had a relationship that went bust only because I found out on social media that he'd gotten married to one of my close friends."

"Yikes."

"I know. And it becomes so hard to trust anyone after going through that. You keep second guessing yourself when someone new comes into your life."

"True, but it's also because of such experiences that I got the chance to meet you."

Becca locked eyes with Max. Here was a good man—kind and wonderful—and she was lucky to have met him.

Max drew her close, and Becca leaned forward. Max brushed away the stray hair from her face, his touch like soft tendrils on her skin. She cared for this man, and that was all the more reason to tell him the truth. "Max—"

A shrill tone pierced the air. Max pulled out his phone and looked at the screen. He frowned and then answered the phone. He listened for a few minutes.

"I'll be right there," he responded.

~

They rode back in silence and reached the barn before long. Max had called for a ranch hand, and he handed the horses over to him.

They strode over to the main house. Becca wondered what had happened. She hoped all was well.

Soon a courier standing in front of the house came into view.

"Hi. I'm Max Dexin," he said to the thin young man.

"You have a delivery, sir. Could you sign here, please?" the man said.

Max signed, and then the delivery guy handed him an envelope. The man jumped into his car and sped off.

Max waited till he entered the house before ripping the envelope open. A single sheet fluttered to the floor. He picked it up and read the note. His face darkened, but he said nothing.

"What is it?" Becca asked, putting a hand on his arm.

"I need to go and see someone in town. I'll be back later."

"Is everything alright? How can I help?"

"I'll be back soon, okay?"

He turned and headed toward the attached garage.

Becca stood and watched him leave. She hoped all was well. It appeared it wasn't something he was willing to share, but she would wait till he was ready.

But she'd lost the opportunity to tell him the secret that haunted her.

Becca tried to work on her wedding planning to-dos, but she couldn't concentrate. She was worried about Max. He still wasn't back. She'd tried to call his number, but it went straight to voicemail. Becca hoped everything was okay.

Maggie and Chloe were still not back from grocery shopping, and Chloe felt restless. So she donned her boots and headed outside. Maybe feeding Bella and rubbing her down would take away some of the anxiety.

She walked out of the house and strode to the barn. She walked past some of the other horses till she reached Bella. She'd brought treats, and she offered Bella a carrot and apple which she gobbled up.

Becca picked up a brush from the supplies room and began to brush her coat down. The mindless activity calmed her, and she prayed for Max. She hoped all would be well.

Then she heard a sound and turned. Becca was surprised to see the woman she'd met at the church walking toward her. She dropped the brush and left Bella's stall, securing it behind her. "What are you doing here?" she asked.

The woman gave a brittle laugh. "I should be asking you that. Why are you in Max's home?"

Of all the nerve. Who did this woman think she was? "I believe it's none of your business," Becca said.

"You weren't supposed to be there, you know."

What was this woman talking about?

"In Las Vegas. You weren't supposed to meet him."

How did this woman know about Vegas? And that was when Becca noticed the tattoo at her collarbone, and it all came crashing back. This was the waitress that had served them the drinks—the person she'd been looking for.

"He was supposed to be alone in that restaurant," the woman said.

Becca noticed that her eyes were wild—this woman was dangerous. She looked around for anything she could use as a weapon and saw a manure fork resting against the wall. She had to keep the woman talking to reach it.

"The plan had been to spike his drink, get him to pass out, and then take care of him till morning. Then he would have been mine," the woman said. "It was supposed to be easy and simple, and I had everything ready. But you had to show up and mess everything up." By this time, the woman was breathing hard.

Becca inched her way slowly to where the manure fork lay. She just had to keep her engaged a few more minutes, and then she would have the weapon in her hands.

"You had to end up with him. And instead of treasuring him, you broke his heart! I tried to stop him from racing after you from the hotel, I really did, but you were all he was interested in. You destroyed him, abandoned him for many years, and when he had gotten over what you had done, you had the nerve to come back, and bring a brat along."

The words were like broken glass, driving shards of pain into Becca's heart, and she gasped. It was true, all of it had been her fault.

"Well, I'm not going to give you any chance to do that. I sent him on a fool's errand, with a note that Tammy was back and wanted to speak with him. Of course, he would rush over—he loved her for many years. I needed to get you all alone to be able to get rid of you."

"But why Max? What has he ever done to you?"

"Max saved me when my father used to beat me like a dog everyday. The man would use whatever he got his hands on. Max made sure he went to jail. He promised me he would make sure that I was okay and found a family to take care of me. Well, now I'm a big girl, and I'm good enough for him. How am I supposed to be alright when he keeps liking other women?"

This lady was delusional. She'd turned Max's kindness into something evil. She needed to be stopped.

Becca neared the fork. Two more steps, and then she would have it in her hand.

"Don't you dare take another step, or I'll

shoot." Becca looked up to see the woman brandishing a pistol.

Her heart galloped, but she managed to keep her breathing even. "What do you want?"

"I want to burn this barn and burn you down with it. I have to get rid of you to get my chance."

A cold dread crawled its way around Becca's heart. One look into the woman's eyes and she knew she could do it. But first, Becca had to save the horses. "Why don't you let the horses go? It's really me you want."

The woman laughed, the noise grating on Becca's nerves. "You think I don't know what you are up to? You are trying to find a way to save yourself."

These horses were Max's pride and joy. He would be devastated if anything happened to them. Becca had to try and save them. "What if you watch me and shoot if I make any sudden movements? You know Max loves these horses, and he would never be with you if they died."

She saw the look of uncertainty cross the woman's face. *Please God, let her agree.*

"Okay, but you have five minutes to get them out, otherwise they die with you."

Becca hurried over to each stall and coaxed each horse to come out and leave the barn.

"You have three minutes." It was obvious the woman was enjoying what was happening. There were a few stragglers, but Becca pulled on their lead ropes and managed to send them walking out of the barn.

"One minute." Two more horses were left. Becca hit their rumps, and they galloped out of the area.

She heard a click and turned. The woman was by the entrance and shot at her. Becca dove down, her heart beating fast in her chest.

The woman let out a maniacal laugh and then shot a can in the corner of the barn. The can exploded, and the smell of gasoline filled the air. She shot again and the hay underneath it caught fire and spread quickly. "Goodbye, Rebecca," she said as she slammed the barn shut.

Becca raced to the main doors but couldn't reach them before the flames rose in front of her. She staggered backward and then she tripped over something on the floor and went down. Becca felt a sharp pain in her arm from where she'd landed.

She couldn't die like this. She still had Chloe

to take care of, family and friends that loved her, and Max who she'd been given a second chance with.

She pushed herself up, cradled her arm, and hurried as much as she could to the second exit. It was locked securely. She grabbed a wheel barrow that was parked in a corner and used it to ram the door, but it didn't budge. Instead, the pain in her arm intensified from the effort.

By now, smoke had filled the barn, and she started coughing. She tore the bottom of her dress and searched for a bucket of water, which she found in one of the stalls. She dipped the piece of cloth into it and covered her nose and mouth. *God, please save me!*

The sound of crackling beams crashing down was the last thing Becca heard before her world turned black.

CHAPTER 29

Max drove up the driveway back to the main house. He'd gone to the coffee shop that Tammy was supposed to meet him in and waited. But no one showed up. And there had been no message left for him either. It had been a wasted trip.

Then he looked up and saw smoke spiraling into the air. Was that fire? It couldn't be. They had just installed the latest sprinkler equipment against that likelihood.

Then he saw the horses spooked and sprinting in his direction. He quickly parked his truck and hopped out. He rounded the corner and saw some of his ranch hands trying to pull the horses away and bring them under control, while others were spraying water over the barn.

Max ran forward till he met his ranch manager. "What happened?" he asked.

"We don't know," the man responded. "We just saw the fire from a distance and ran over here to control it. Dex and Jax are trying to get Bella away from the other side of the barn, but she's digging in, and we don't know why."

Max raced to the other side, only to see Bella going wild as they tried to control her. He soon reached her and tried to calm her down.

"Thank goodness you're here," Dex said. "We were finding it harder and harder to rein her in."

Max rubbed her side. "What is it, Bella?"

Bella neighed and made to go in the direction of the barn. Dex and Max held her back. There was one thing Max knew about Bella—she was loyal to a fault. The only way she would be heading toward a fire was if there was something or someone important to him who was in there.

"Did all the horses get out?" Max asked Dex.

"Yes, they did."

"What about people? Anyone working here missing?"

"No, all are accounted for."

The only folks Bella cared about were the ones that fed him, Max, and ... His heart quickened. "Has anyone seen Becca?"

"Becca?" Dex asked. "Isn't she supposed to be in the house?"

"She wasn't at home," Jax said. "I thought she went out with Maggie to the grocery store."

A cold fear gripped Max's heart. Becca was inside. That was what Bella was trying to tell them. He couldn't let anything happen to her. He picked up two blankets lying on the floor and dunked them in water one after the other. "Only Chloe went to the store. She is in there. That's why Bella wasn't budging."

"You can't go in there, Max," Dex said. "The fire department is almost here." Max could hear their siren drawing closer.

"I can't wait." He threw one blanket over himself and then ran into the burning barn.

Thick smoke filled his view as he jumped over the barn door that had collapsed from the flame. He coughed and then covered his nose with the wet blanket and screamed her name. "Becca!"

There was no response. The flames licked up one side of the top beam, and he could see it threatening to collapse. Then he saw a glimpse of the dress she'd worn earlier today.

"Becca," he screamed and pushed the debris away not caring if it burned his hands till he got to where she lay unconscious on the floor. He heard a groaning sound and looked up to see the beams crashing down toward where she lay.

Max flew over and covered her with his body as the beams landed all over him.

That was the last thing he remembered before his vision narrowed and then dimmed.

Becca opened her eyes to see herself in a room that looked similar to the VIP hospital room she'd been in recently. She tried to sit up, but her whole body ached and she fell back against the pillows.

"She's awake," a voice that sounded like Leah's said, and soon her face and Jasmine's came into view.

"Thank you, God," Jasmine said. "How are you feeling?"

"Like there's cotton in my mouth," Becca said. "Where am I?"

"In Dexington Medical Center," Jasmine responded.

She'd guessed as much. "What about Chloe?"

"Dana took her to get some ice-cream," Jasmine said. "She's fine."

Then Becca remembered the fire. "Is everyone safe? What about the horses?"

"Calm down," Leah said. "The horses are fine. You had a mild concussion, but there was no fracture. Only some first-degree burns, which the doctors expect to heal quickly."

"Was there anyone else hurt?"

Leah and Jasmine looked at each other and said nothing.

Becca's pulse rate increased. "What is it? What are you hiding from me?" she asked.

"We have to tell her," Jasmine said. "It's Max. He ran in to save you and was the only reason you escaped relatively unscathed. But one of the beams hit his head, and he is currently unconscious."

Becca struggled to get up. "I have to see him."

"Take it easy, Becca," Leah said. "He's in the ICU and in the hands of professionals."

"I have to see him," Becca said, her voice breaking. "Don't you understand?"

Becca sat in the wheelchair and watched Max as he lay motionless on the ICU hospital bed. The doctors had given her permission to visit him for a few minutes.

A tube snaked into his mouth held in place by strips of tape. His torso was wrapped in bandages, and an IV line connected to his arm was in place. His chest rose and fell as the bedside monitors beeped rhythmically.

Max had suffered the brunt of the injury on his back with some second-degree burns—a wet blanket he'd thrown over his body had saved him from further harm. The doctors had been amazed that he sustained no fractures to his back or limbs—it could only be a miracle.

A section of a beam had hit his head, and the doctors weren't certain yet whether he'd sustained any brain damage. The medical staff had provided the basic emergency care he'd needed, and now it was a waiting game.

"We have to go," a nurse whispered in Becca's ear.

Becca wheeled her chair forward till she was close to the bed. She took his free hand and held it in her hands. She leaned forward. "Max, please wake up. Your whole family is waiting for you. I'm waiting for you. I'm so sorry it's all my fault. Please wake up. I love you." She raised his hand to her lips and kissed it. Then she laid it back on the bed gently.

She nodded to the nurse, who turned the chair and wheeled her out of the ICU.

CHAPTER 31

The intermittent beeping from the monitors pierced the fog that clouded Max's mind. He forced his eyes open to see harsh white light shining down from the ceiling above. He squeezed his eyes shut and then opened them again. Now, it didn't hurt as much.

Max tried to speak, but a tube in his mouth stimulated the gag reflex, and he lifted his arm to pull it out.

"He's awake," he heard a voice say. And then there was a flurry of activities around him.

"Dr. Dexin, can you hear us? If you can, blink twice."

Max blinked twice with as much effort as he could muster.

"Awesome."

Max was certain he'd heard Becca's voice, telling him to wake up. But where was she? He tried to move his head, but it hurt so much and he let out a groan.

Then he felt the fog pulling him back, and his eyes closed.

Max sat up on his hospital bed and stared out the window. He'd made a speedy recovery once he had been considered stable enough to transfer to the VIP wing. He'd had a mild concussion, and the burns on his back were expected to heal well with treatment.

The detectives had come and gone. They had informed Max that the fire had been arson instead of an accident—someone had purposely cut off the sprinkler system and set the place on fire—and the culprit had been caught.

Max was surprised at who it was. He'd helped the girl out of the kindness of his heart, yet she'd put everything he considered important at risk. Thank goodness the main house hadn't been affected. They were going to spend a lot of money to rebuild the barn, but no human lives were lost, and all the horses were safe. It was only God's mercies, and Max was grateful.

But one good thing had come of the incident. He'd recovered his lost memory—how he'd met Becca and how he'd chased after her the next day and ended up in an accident. He still didn't recall what happened that fateful night and he probably never would—the lady had confessed to spiking his drinks in Vegas, one of which Becca had consumed. So there was no point in stressing about it any longer.

But what was most painful was Becca had recognized him the whole time she'd stayed in his home and had watched him make a fool of himself. And after he'd thought about it and done his calculations, he'd determined that Chloe was most likely his child. All he needed was a DNA test to confirm it. Becca had known, and yet she'd allowed Chloe to address him like a stranger.

She'd had many chances to tell him the truth, yet she hadn't. Most likely because she didn't trust him. He'd foolishly opened his heart to her, and she had stomped it into the ground.

As much as he hated to do so, he had to give

her a chance to explain why. And then he needed some time before he could decide what to do next.

The door creaked open, and he turned in that direction.

"Hello, Max."

The moment had arrived.

It was time to find out the truth.

CHAPTER 32

Becca stood at the entrance to Max's hospital room. She'd heard he had regained consciousness and was now in the VIP wing. And she'd known she couldn't put off the visit any longer.

Her heart skipped a beat, and her throat went dry. She was afraid to face him, yet she had no choice. She forced herself to take one step and then another as she approached him. Max's eyes never left hers, his face remaining impassive.

"Hello, Max," she said again as she stopped a few feet from where he sat.

"Please sit," he responded.

Becca settled with relief into one of the visitor's chairs. She got tired easily since the incident, but the doctors had assured her she would regain her full strength in a few weeks.

The silence between them eventually became uncomfortable. She would have to speak now, or she might lose her courage.

"I'm sorry," Becca said.

The words hung heavy in the air between them, but Max said nothing.

She had to continue. "I'm sorry I didn't say anything about meeting you in Vegas. I'd heard it was best for amnesiac patients to recover their memory on their own, and I didn't want to taint it."

She swallowed. Now, she had to address the elephant in the room. She couldn't meet his gaze. "And I'm sorry for not telling you about Chloe. That she was your child."

"Look at me," Max said quietly.

Becca lifted her eyes and stared into his. Instead of anger, she saw sorrow and distress.

Her heart squeezed in pain. She had done this. She had shattered his heart over and over again.

"Becca, I deserved to know she was my daughter. From the moment we met again, you had many chances to let me know. We even kissed, yet you didn't tell me."

"I'm sorry." Tears stung behind her eyelids, but Becca forced them back. She didn't deserve to cry.

"Chloe must have been missing her dad, and I was right there in front of her, yet you watched her treat me like a stranger. Not only did you hurt me, you hurt our daughter!"

"I'm so sorry," she said in a tremulous voice.

Max sighed. "When were you planning to tell me?" he asked wearily.

"At the picnic. But then you got the call about the package, and it didn't happen."

He ran a hand through his hair. "This is all too much for me right now. I need some time to think about everything. I think it might be best for you to stay with your sister in Dexington. I'll reach out once I'm ready to talk."

She nodded. As much as it hurt her, she knew it made total sense.

He looked at her. "I'm glad you are okay. Take care of yourself, Becca."

Max turned and faced the window again.

The conversation was over.

Becca got up and left the room.

She'd crushed the heart of the man she loved, and her heart had lost in the process.

It had been two weeks, and Becca's life had returned to some normalcy. The paparazzi had gotten tired of hanging around and had disappeared. Now she could walk the streets and not worry about being recognized. Her burns had healed completely, and she had regained her energy. Her assistant had even resumed work, and together they had made progress on the triple wedding plans. Every other aspect of her life was going well. But Becca's heart was empty.

She missed Max. Her heart was at the ranch, where he was. Becca had heard nothing from him, and her heart sank a little lower with each day that passed. She thought about him day and night. Every smile from Chloe even reminded her of him. Chloe was also constantly asking about him and when she would see him again.

Becca got up and stared out the window of the home office that Leah had created for her. The door opened behind her, and she turned to see Leah enter the room. Becca turned back to the window. Leah soon stood beside her.

"How are you doing?" Leah asked.

"I've gotten a lot of the wedding planning done. Even Sarah Dexington is happy with what I have accomplished."

"You know that's not what I'm talking about."

Becca inhaled and then exhaled. "I don't know," she said quietly.

Leah turned and faced her. "So what are you going to do about it?"

"I don't know. I have to wait and give him time. I can't just go and look for him."

"Why not? It's been two weeks—men do not need more thinking time than that." Leah forced Becca to face her. "Listen, I know you've made mistakes, grave ones, but it's time to move on beyond that. You and Max are bound by Chloe, and nothing can change that. Even if he's not ready to make a decision about your relationship with him, he needs to establish a relationship with Chloe before she gets hurt." She let go of Becca. "Do you want him back in your lives?"

"Yes. I miss him."

"Then, pack your bags and get going!"

A knock sounded on the door. The door opened, and one of Leah's assistants poked her head in.

"What is it?" Leah asked.

"There is a Max Dexin looking for Miss Scott."

CHAPTER 33

"Max, stop pacing!" Dex said. "You're making me see stars."

Max turned to Dex. "I'm sorry. What was it you said again?"

"We were talking about the ER center. Did you get a chance to discuss it with Blake?"

"Yes, I did. He's pitching it to the board next week, but he's already put feelers out, and it has been all positive feedback so far."

"What about the modification on the architectural plans?" Dex asked.

"What did you say?"

"Max!"

"I'm sorry."

"See? You need to go get her."

Max sighed and sat down at his desk. "I'm not sure if I'm ready."

"Of course, you'll never be ready. Fine, she made a big mistake, but it wasn't exactly easy for her. It's not like you dropped your address when you were leaving Vegas. And she raised your child for four years, a child that has turned out to be one of the most delightful kids you'll ever know." Dex twirled his pen. "And finally, you're not getting younger. You better go after her before she changes her mind."

"Thanks for rubbing the age factor in my face," Max said.

"You're welcome."

He thought for a moment. "But I'm not sure if she wants to stay on the ranch."

"Then build two homes, one here and one in Dexington. Don't you love her enough to make the sacrifice?"

He leaned back. Dex was right. Even though she'd hurt him, he couldn't imagine anyone else in his life apart from her. It was time to put the old behind and start anew. And there was no time to waste.

CHAPTER 34

"Hello, Max," Becca said. She looked thinner than the last time he'd seen her. They stood under the gazebo in Leah's garden. It was private enough without any ears listening in on their conversation. "You look well."

"You too," he responded. There was no need to beat about the bush.

"Rebecca Scott, would you marry me?"

Becca gasped. It was clear she wasn't expecting that.

"And no, it's not because I'm Chloe's father," he was quick to reassure her. "You drive me crazy sometimes, but I love you just the way you are. And I adore you as the mother of my child. Could we start all over again?"

Becca laughed. He'd missed the sound. "I'm dumbfounded," she said.

"But …"

"I'm happy. Yes, I would love for us to start all over again. And yes, I will marry you."

'Woohoo!" Max picked her up and twirled her around.

Becca flushed, and her ears turned red. "Put me down, Max."

"Sorry," he said sheepishly. "But I'm not done yet." He fished out a set of keys and handed them over to her. "Here are the keys to our new house."

"House? I thought we already had one at the ranch."

"But I know your work will bring you into the city, and I'd sometimes have to come here myself. So I bought the house across the street."

"You mean—"

"Yep, you and your sister are neighbors. I assumed you'd want that more than any other location."

Becca's eyes brimmed with tears. "Don't worry, I'm not crying," she said.

"I love you, Becca Scott," he said tenderly.

He could see the love shining in her eyes. "I love you, Max Dexin."

And then Max held her in his arms and gave her a kiss he was sure she felt all the way to the tip of her toes.

"Next!" The loud voice of the clerk in city hall echoed in the room.

It was their turn. Max and Becca walked up to the counter. "We'd like to apply for a marriage license," Max said. Max and Becca had dated for three months and had decided they wanted to just get a marriage license and then have a huge reception with family and friends.

"Have you filled out the application form and paid the fee?" the clerk asked.

"Yes, we have," Becca said. "Here it is."

She passed the form and receipt to the clerk.

The clerk typed some information into the computer, read the screen, and looked quizzically at them. She typed it in yet again.

Then she leaned back and threw her hands up in the air. "Are you kidding me?"

Max and Becca entered the barn where the reception was taking place. They had rebuilt a new one, and Becca had requested an extension that could be converted to an event hall. Max had granted her request.

Family and friends from the area and from Dexington filled the space, which was decorated in both jewel and earthy tones. Becca had also wanted a touch of the old with the new, so photos from the mantel in the main house had been placed around the room. She noticed Grandma Helen, Blake's grandmother, studying the wagon picture Alicia had spotted before.

"Oh my goodness," Grandma Helen said, and placed a hand against her heart.

"What is it, Grandma?" Blake asked.

Grandma Helen turned to Dex who was also standing close. "I can't believe this," she said to him. Then she grabbed him and gave him a kiss on the cheek.

Dex turned tomato-red. Everyone around them looked on in shock.

"Grandma, are you okay?" Alicia asked.

"My dear, I can't help it since I just found our long-lost relatives! I need to sit down."

Blake rushed and placed a seat behind her, and she sat down. Family and friends seated around the tables quietened as they waited eagerly for Grandma Helen to continue.

"My father-in-law showed me this picture when I just married into the family. We have a copy on our mantel at home. He said it was a picture of the families when they first arrived in America. But the Dexington cousins wanted a good place to breed horses and such, so they left in a wagon in search of some good land. But that was the last they ever heard of them. They must have shortened their last name to Dexin."

Becca glanced at Max who was in shock. She squeezed his arm reassuringly. Now he had a whole extra family that he never knew existed.

"Come here," Grandma Helen said to Dex, who approached with trepidation. She grabbed him into a tight embrace.

"Grandma, I can't breathe," Dex said.

"Toughen it up, cowboy!"

The whole room collapsed in laughter. Max let out a guffaw.

That was when Blake noticed Becca and Max were in the barn. "Hey, you're back."

All eyes turned on them. "Congratulations!" the room shouted as one.

Becca stiffened, and her face fell. Max reacted the same.

Their guests noticed the change in Max's and Becca's facial expressions.

Leah hurried forward. "What's wrong? What's with the long face?"

Becca sighed. "We couldn't get the marriage license."

A silence dominated the room. Everyone in the hall looked at each other. This was not good.

"Why?" Maggie asked. She was dressed in a dusky-pink mother-of-the-groom dress.

"We can't get married," Max said.

A murmur ran through the crowd.

"Why not?" Grandma Helen asked. "Come on, spit it out already."

"Because we're ALREADY MARRIED!" Max and Becca shouted in unison.

The whole room gasped. "What?" Jasmine said.

Max had a cheesy smile on his face. "We got married five years ago in Vegas," Max said. "We've been married this whole time and didn't know it!"

Blake laughed. "You're kidding!"

Jax shook his head in disbelief. "How can you not know you're married?"

"Because our drinks got spiked, and we couldn't remember what happened that night," Becca said.

"And we don't know what happened to the keepsake certificate," Max finished.

"So what do we call what we're doing now?" asked Josh, Dana's fiancé.

"Hmm. Their fifth anniversary reception?" David, Jasmine's fiancé, suggested.

"Whatever we call it, we need to make it quick," Willow, Alicia's daughter, said.

"Why?" Blake asked.

Willow shook her head in disbelief that no one had figured that out. "Duh, Dad, because they have five years to make up for!" She grabbed Chloe's hand. "Come on, Chloe."

The whole room erupted in laughter.

Becca smiled as she leaned against Max.

There was no other place she'd rather be than here.

Her wedding planning business had grown by leaps and bounds, and the Dexington Health-care Board had approved the collaboration with the Dexin ER Center. Construction work had already begun, and Max had his hands full as the Interim Director of the center. Chloe was thriving with family and friends around her, and their move to the ranch had been smooth.

Becca's heart was full.

Because she had come home.

To her very own Billionaire Cowboy Doc.

Thank you so much for reading! Want to know what happens next in Dexington, and how Dex, Max's brother, found love with a doctor (in a blind date romance)?

Check out A DOCTOR BLIND DATE FOR THE COWBOY at https://dobidaniels.com.

Here's an excerpt:

Zoey Brown froze, her face warming up

more than the hot Saturday summer sun she'd just walked in from. How could this have happened to her today of all days?

"Ma'am, your skirt has a problem," the cool baritone voice repeated quietly behind her.

Zoey bristled even as the scented smell of cleaning supplies from the nearby detergent aisle assaulted her nostrils. Yes, she'd heard him the first time. Did he have to repeat it again? She fought the urge to reach back and touch the rip that had appeared as she'd leaned forward to place her groceries on the checkout counter.

It served her right. She should have just stuck with the slacks and jeans that had been her uniform for over a decade. Instead, she'd opted for a black skirt and a sleeveless peach blouse that went wonderfully with her sun-kissed skin for a change, because today's weather forecast had predicted it would be the hottest day of summer. Who knew the universe would reward her efforts with this unwanted publicity on her first day in Dexin Valley?

Zoey bit her lip. She couldn't continue

standing here, pretending nothing was wrong. How was she going to get herself out of this pickle? Her jacket was in her car, too far away to reach without taking a walk of shame through the store to the parking lot. How could she deal with this in the gracious manner her stepmother liked to harp on, without becoming the day's side show in the tiny grocery store that seemed to be serving half of the town's population today?

Something fell on Zoey's shoulders, and she flinched. Her eyes looked down only to see a dark brown plaid shirt—long enough to extend beyond the hem of her skirt—resting on her shoulders. It held the faint scent of sweet hay, leather, and fresh grass, a fragrance that seemed to warm her more than the shirt itself.

Zoey turned in relief to see who the owner was, and her eyes met the warmest brown eyes she'd ever seen, twin mirrors that seemed to reach down into her soul. The broad-chested young man towered over her five-foot-seven frame, and his eyes held a look of concern as they searched her face.

"Are you okay, ma'am?" he asked in the same voice she'd heard earlier...

Want to read more? You can grab A DOCTOR BLIND DATE FOR THE COWBOY at https://dobidaniels.com!

Or want to know what happens next in Dexington?
Sign up now at https://dobidaniels.com.

If you've loved reading Loving the Billionaire Cowboy Doc, Dobi would be grateful if you could spend a few minutes to leave a review (as short as you like) on the book's page on your favorite retailer. Your review would help bring it to the attention of other readers. Thank you very much.

Check out all Dobi Daniels books at https://dobidaniels.com

ACKNOWLEDGMENTS

Writing a book is harder and more rewarding than I could have ever imagined. And it would not have been possible without the support, love, and encouragement from my number one cheerleader, my dearest mom. My life would never have been this awesome and wonderful without you.

Of course, I have to thank my precious little DC for his smiles and antics. You brighten my day and give me the strength to keep pushing through.

Thank you to my sisters for encouraging me on this wonderful journey. And a special thanks to my baby brother (who is so not a baby anymore) for being super supportive and checking in on my progress. You guys are the best.

Thank you to my wonderful author friends. You know who you are. Your selflessness and willingness to share what you know has made my writing journey smoother and an exciting one. And a special thanks to Lisa and Deanna whose support have made a difference.

Most of all, I want to thank God who gave me life, surrounded me with the most wonderful people, and loved me all the way. You make my life complete.

And finally, a special thanks to all my readers whose love of my stories spur me on to write more. Thank you!

ABOUT DOBI DANIELS

As a former physician and business executive in another life—with a childhood filled with reading multi-genre novels—Dobi Daniels loves to write sweet thrilling romance stories with heart. She enjoys dreaming up everyday characters who rise above unfavorable circumstances to overcome incredible odds and find joy along the way.

When not writing, Dobi can be found binging K-dramas and ice cream with her little sidekick by her side.

Loving the Billionaire Cowboy Doc is the fifth book in the Dexington Doctor Billionaires Series. Sign up at dobidaniels.com to be notified when the next Dobi Daniels book comes out!

Thank you!

He got up, grabbed his hat from where it hung on the coat rack, and strode out of his office, leaving behind a grinning Dex.